WHATEVER WE ARE

BY
LEIGH FLEMING

Published by Envisage Press, LLC
Copyright © 2017 Envisage Press, LLC
Cover by www.spikyshooz.com

ISBN: 978-0-9977351-5-4

This is a work of fiction. All of the characters, names, incidents, organizations, and dialogue in this novel are either the products of the author's imagination or are used fictitiously.

Also by Leigh Fleming

Precious Words
Whatever You Call Me
Whatever You Say

ONE

The happiest time of year for most people stretched from Thanksgiving dinner until the clock struck midnight on New Year's Eve, but not for Liza Fisk. For Liza, the six weeks of overeating, materialism, and holiday fakery drudged up memories of Christmases gone wrong. It did, however, provide her with a substantial income from the sale of her one-of-a-kind Christmas cards—an irony she chose to ignore.

Sitting at her Aunt Linda's table surrounded by family didn't help her mood; in fact, it only accentuated the impending doom of the season. With a deep eye roll and a heavy sigh, she passed the large platter of white and dark meat to her right and turned to accept a steaming bowl of mashed potatoes from her sister-in-law, Kate. She tugged the silver spoon out of the thick glob of carbs and *thwacked* a hefty pile on her already crowded plate. Every Thanksgiving dinner was the same: after the plates were filled to overflowing, her mother and her aunt would compare their talented, successful children, and Liza would be reminded she didn't quite measure up.

Her beautiful cousin Diana was about to arrive, which put her nerves on edge. Everything Diana touched turned to gold, or so it would seem with the way Aunt Linda bragged. Liza drew in a deep breath, inhaling the savory smell of turkey, stuffing, and other comfort foods that unfortunately gave her little comfort.

"I'm so sorry Diana is running late everyone. Apparently there was a wreck on the interstate, but she insisted we start without her," Aunt

Linda said. The blinding sparkle of her diamond ring was going to set off a migraine. Uncle Rodney's construction business must be paying off big.

"She said she has something exciting to announce when she arrives. She just got that big promotion, so I can't image what else it could be."

Probably something amazing. Diana's life had been flawless from the moment the doctor smacked her cute little behind: from her wealthy daddy to her patrician beauty to her polished persona, she had it all. She was smart, sociable, and ambitious, and Liza had always felt inferior to Diana's perfection. Liza sawed across a thick slice of turkey as if she were cutting through a felled tree and stabbed into the meat, dragging it through the potatoes and gravy before shoving it in her mouth. While her cheeks bulged like a squirrel in winter, her mother picked the worst time to ask a question.

"Liza, would you like to tell everyone about the invitation you received?"

"Hmm?" She really didn't want to talk about it in front of her wildly successful family, so she shoved a dollop of mashed potatoes in her mouth. Maybe if she ate quickly she could get out of there before the comparisons got too deep.

"She's been asked by a prestigious art academy to submit some of her pieces for a juried show." Her mother smiled sweetly as she placed a tiny forkful of peas in her mouth.

"Mawm," Liza complained through the thick glop halfway down her throat.

She wasn't sure she was going to enter. Between work and finishing the last of her Christmas card orders, she hadn't had time to paint. Besides, the invitation wasn't *that* prestigious—just a regional competition. But it gave Sherri something impressive to say about her lackluster daughter.

"How exciting," Aunt Linda said.

"Had enough of bartending yet?" Leave it to Uncle Rodney to remind everyone that Liza worked part-time at the Brass Rail—wasting that college diploma she'd earned.

"What's the name of the competition? And where is it?" Liza suspected Aunt Linda knew she wouldn't enter.

She swallowed the decimated mass of food with a loud gulp and plastered on a smile to match her mother's. "It's in Pittsburgh, but I'm not sure I'll enter." She picked up her glass of sweet tea and took a long drink.

"Pity." Aunt Linda tired of that subject and went back to her favorite. "Diana just got a big raise, did I tell you? Her promotion to assistant vice president came with a lot of perks."

The annual Thanksgiving Day Comparison Olympics was in full swing. Already, Aunt Linda had earned a gold medal on behalf of Diana. After a lifetime of one-upping each other, one would think her mom and her aunt would get bored with it all. Her aunt had plenty to brag about: her daughter Tera worked for a big-name fashion house in New York City, and Diana was quickly climbing the corporate ladder at the biggest bank in their home state of West Virginia. Of course, Mom had earned a few gold medals in the past because of Liza's brother, Brody, winner of several CMA and Grammy awards from his successful songwriting career. In addition to that, he had recently married Kate and they had their first child two months ago. Liza's only major accomplishment was one lousy art prize she had won in college. Besides making the best margarita in Highland Springs, her parents had little to brag about when it came to her accomplishments. But, that would soon change. She had bigger dreams than a regional art competition, plans that would have everyone talking *and* bring a much needed dose of culture to this town.

She stuffed a buttery roll into her mouth, hoping her chewing would block out the chatter, as the front door blasted open on a rush of cool autumn air. Diana Murray was home.

"We made it." Diana threw open her arms, smiling as if the paparazzi were waiting, and released an annoying giggle. "I hope you saved some for us."

Uncle Rodney rushed from the head of the table and gathered his little girl in his arms, followed by the rest of the Murray clan who swallowed her in hugs and kisses. Liza hadn't figured out what Diana meant by "we," but could see a dark head peeking from behind.

Finally, the waters parted and her cousin stepped forward with the other half of "we," his hands firmly placed on her cashmere-clad shoulders. Liza asphyxiated on her iced tea and coughed up what was left in her throat.

"This is my big surprise. You remember Bret Bridges." Liza slapped the pilgrim-adorned napkin against her mouth and held back a deep belly laugh. Bret Bridges, crowned Mr. Highland Springs his senior year, was from the wealthiest family in the county. He was a carbon copy of Diana—another golden child—handsome, charming, and politician smooth.

And the first boy to break Liza's heart. She should have known they'd eventually end up together.

First semester of Liza's high school junior year, Bret, a senior, sat beside her in art class. Up until that time, he had never spoken to her, but soon they stayed after school to work on projects together and occasionally he'd call her at night. She fell, hard and fast, and that major crush lasted more than a year but ended in humiliation, heartbreak, and a ride in an ambulance. Seeing Bret sent a cold shiver down her spine, reminiscent of the icy roads that put her in the hospital through Christmas day that year.

"Aunt Sherri, Uncle Doug, you remember Bret, don't you?" Diana led Bret by the nose—well, the elbow—re-introducing him to everyone around the table while Liza plowed through her plate so she could get the heck out of there. She had just swallowed a mouthful of stuffing when hands grasped her shoulders. She turned and found Diana's heavily lined eyes glistening only inches from her own. She dug her nails into Liza's arms and tugged her into a brief hug.

"Lizard, it's been so long." Why couldn't Diana drop that silly child-hood name? "You remember Bret, don't you?"

Liza glanced over Diana's shoulder and found Bret smiling like a game show host about to give away a side-by-side refrigerator freezer.

"Of course she does. How've you been, Liza?"

He wrenched her out of Diana's embrace, pulled her to her feet, and smothered her in a bear hug. His cologne was heavy, burning the back of her throat, making it hard to breathe.

"Still got that funky artist vibe going on, I see."

She stepped out of his arms and brushed her long hair over her shoulder, suddenly self-conscience of the blue tint she'd applied this morning.

"Liza has a unique style that represents her multitude of talents."

Really, Mom? Was she so pathetic her mother needed to defend her choice of hair color and fashion sense? And since when did she have a multitude of talents? Admittedly, she was an excellent painter and a whiz with a cocktail shaker, but declaring she had numerous talents was a bit of a stretch unless you counted her gift for matchmaking and her killer baking skills. Those two abilities were universally known.

"I've been great, Bret. Good to see you, too." She plopped into her seat and stared at the near-empty plate. Would anyone notice if she had another helping of mashed potatoes?

"Come you two. Come sit by me." Aunt Linda waved Diana and Bret toward her end of the table, pointing a long, tapered fingernail at two chairs beside her. "This is such a nice surprise. You hinted at a new man in your life."

Unlike Diana who seemed to have a new boyfriend every season, Liza had remained single, enjoying her unencumbered freedom. She had an active social life with plenty of friends, and didn't need a man to complete her.

"So tell me everything. What have I missed by living in Charleston?" Diana cast the question out to the table hoping someone would bite. What she got in return were a few *wells* and *ums*, nothing worth reeling in.

"How about you Liza? Still painting I presume?"

"Yep. Just shipped out my last Christmas card order."

"That's so nice."

Diana's sickeningly sweet reply was anything but. She had no idea the work that went into making the exclusive watercolor cards. Liza started in February, creating six custom designs, and each year she gained new customers. If business continued growing at its current rate, she would have to find another artist to help fill the orders. Her cards were truly unique and earned her almost enough money to live. Bartending at the Brass Rail made up the difference, and kept her up to date with news around town.

"Your Aunt Sherri told us she's in a huge art competition," Aunt Linda said with a condescending smile.

"I wouldn't call it—"

"How exciting. When do you have time to paint and make cards? Don't you still work at the Brass Rail?" Diana asked with a sneer.

"Well, I only—"

"Whatever happened to your gallery idea?" With Bret's question came a stunned silence. How did he remember the dream she'd shared with him back in high school—a dream she hadn't even shared with her family?

"A gallery?" Mom's sweet potatoes stopped midway to her mouth. "What's this about a gallery?"

"It's something I've always wanted to do."

"A gallery? Here in Highland Springs?" Diana's condescending glare, through narrowed lashes, made the hairs stand up on Liza's neck. Her cousin dismissed the notion with a chuckle and a wave of her hand. Did she think the people of Highland Springs weren't cultured enough to support a gallery? Or did she think Liza wasn't capable of running one?

"Highland Springs is becoming a real tourist town with all the antique stores and great places to eat." Until this moment, Brody had remained silent. "Think of all the folks that come here to hike and raft. And there's the college. Students could benefit from a gallery. There are plenty of people who would love to visit a gallery during their weekend stay."

"Who better than Liza to open such a place?" Kate turned her way, a warm smile on her face. "After all, she knows just about every artist in the state."

If it wouldn't make a scene, Liza would kiss Brody and Kate for their vote of confidence. They must have sensed her frustration, rushing in to save her from the doubters around the table.

"Where will it be? When will it open?" Diana just wouldn't let this go. "How will you pay for it?"

"It's really too soon to talk about."

Liza didn't need her big-mouthed aunt and cousin knowing about her plan to purchase the old castle from the town and turn it into a gallery. The gossip mill in Highland Springs spun so quickly, she purposely had chosen to work with a Pittsburgh design firm on drawings for renovations and talk with several out-of-town banks about financing. The beautiful castle, built by her great-grandfather as the first car dealership in town, had languished in disrepair for decades. The dilapidated home of Camelot Motors had become the brunt of many jokes over the years with such clever monikers as Leaks-a-Lot, Costs-a-Lot, and Mice-a-Lot, to name a few. She was determined to restore it to its original grandeur and redeem her great-grandfather's good name, and at the same time prove to her family she could be a success in the art world.

"Enough about Liza. Let's hear all about the two of you." Kate deflected the attention off Liza, thank God.

For the next ten minutes, the table was entertained with the *delightful* story of how Bret had come into the bank where Diana worked and applied for a loan, reuniting their old friendship after almost eight years. That one loan application turned into dinner and dancing, followed by true love. Two souls destined to become one.

"And I have some even bigger news." Diana clapped her manicured hands together and plastered on a pageant smile until the room became silent. "We're moving back to Highland Springs." She turned and covered her mother's hands with her own. "I didn't tell you, mama, but the promotion I got was to become regional manager for all the branches in the area. I'm moving back to Highland Springs for good."

"Darling, that's wonderful." Aunt Linda gathered Diana in a hug and swiped an errant tear from her cheek. "It will be so nice having you back in your old room."

"Actually, Bret and I are renting a house over on Spruce. He's transferring to the Bridgeport office."

The surprises just kept coming. The next thing Liza expected to hear was they were planning a wedding.

"We're so excited. We'll be settled in our house just in time for Christmas."

Ah, Christmas…that magical time of year when expectations ran high only to be dragged down by disappointment. More suicides happened during the holidays and Liza understood why. Most of her memorable Christmases were best forgotten.

"And we're going to offer our services to be Mr. & Mrs. Claus this year."

"You can't." Liza nearly jumped out of her chair. Highland Springs' Mr. and Mrs. Claus was bestowed on a prominent couple each year and damned if she would let them be chosen.

"Why not?" Diana looked as though she'd been slapped.

"Because…"

It had been offered to Tucker, but he had turned it down, citing the fact that he didn't have a special someone in his life to play the missus.

"…it's already been given to someone one."

"Who?"

"Tucker Callum is going to be Santa this year." Now Tucker had to do it. She wouldn't be able to get through the already nauseating holiday season if Diana and Bret showed up at every local event for the next four weeks. With Tucker's popularity and Liza's matchmaking skills, he should have no problem finding his Christmas sidekick.

"I heard he turned it down," Aunt Linda said with a twist of her lips.

"He's not even dating anyone, is he?" Diana's wine glass sang out a high-pitched tone as she dragged her finger around the rim.

"No, he isn't. The only reason he was chosen is because he fits the part." Aunt Linda's chuckle made Liza's skin crawl. She glanced over at Brody and saw storm clouds forming in his eyes. He was very protective of those he loved and Aunt Linda was close to waking the slumbering bear. She shouldn't be fooled by Brody's laid-back country boy shtick.

"Mr. and Mrs. Claus have always been the town's *it* couple. With this being the thirtieth anniversary of the Mistletoe Ball, you would think the committee would've chosen more wisely. Think how many proposals have happened at the ball over the years. The whole town will be let down if Tucker does it." Diana had stepped onto her soapbox, letting her turkey and stuffing grow cold. "I mean, who wants a Santa without a Mrs. Claus? Folks around here wouldn't stand for it."

"There's nothing in the rule book that says Mr. Claus has to pop the question at the ball," Brody said through clenched teeth. "Besides I think Tucker will be a great Santa."

"Like I said, he fits the part." Aunt Linda bit into a roll with a satisfied snort.

"Have you seen him lately?" Liza fought to keep her butt in her chair. "Tucker has lost a lot of weight. He looks amazing. What do you have against him?"

"It's just, like I said, it's best if Mr. Claus has a Mrs. Claus." Diana laid her hand on Bret's arm and gave him one of her Miss America smiles.

"Tucker will represent Highland Springs well. He loves Christmas, knows just about everyone, and has done a lot for the community. Maybe this year we'll just have Santa and no Mrs. Claus," Brody said.

"That can't be. There has always been a missus for the mister. If he is going to do it he has to designate his Mrs. Claus by tomorrow night at the community center fundraiser," Diana said.

Liza wasn't sure how much longer she could listen to Diana's rant about the current Santa situation. She had to find a way to shut her up.

"Tomorrow night I'm going to talk to the committee members and tell them Bret and I would be honored to represent the town by acting as Mr. and Mrs. Claus during this year's Christmas season. We have to continue the tradition, especially since it's the thirtieth anniversary."

All at once, everyone had an opinion, speaking over one another until Liza thought her head would explode. There was no way in Toyland she would let these two annoyingly perfect people take away Tucker's turn at Santa. The committee had overwhelmingly nominated him and he was looking forward to it—he just didn't know it yet. All this chatter had to stop. Liza rose from her chair and held her arms out to silence the angry mob.

"Listen…shh…I wasn't going to announce this here—it was going to be revealed tomorrow night."

Finally, the clamor settled and Liza had everyone's full attention. Her stomach clenched as she glanced around the table, catching the eager expressions on their faces. This impulse of hers better work.

"Tucker definitely plans to do it and he's chosen his Mrs. Claus."

"He has? But who?" Disappointment drained the flush from Diana's cheeks.

"I promised I wouldn't tell. He'll announce it tomorrow night at the fundraiser."

Actually, Tucker would probably kill her tomorrow night, but Liza had to make sure Diana and Bret wouldn't become Mr. and Mrs. Claus.

Two

Tucker squatted behind the makeshift bar and lifted the keg into the cooler. Tonight was the annual *Bag a Bachelor or Bachelorette* fundraiser where single men and women volunteered to be auctioned off to the highest silent bidder for a date, all to raise money for the community center. Each year the event got bigger and had actually resulted in a few marriages, including Brody and Kate. Tucker had always been too self-conscious of his weight to participate, preferring to stay behind the bar, serving his beer to the locals. Besides, there was only one woman who he'd bid on and she wasn't signed up for the auction.

"Hey, bud, did you bring the new brew you were telling me about?" The tool belt around Travis's waist clanged as he crossed the community center activity room. "I think I earned a pint after all the work I put in here today."

Tucker leaned his elbows on the counter and admired the decorations through the pass-through window. Travis had helped the fundraising committee transform the room into a winter's love nest with white-lit Christmas trees and snowflake garland. Snowy doves and glittered hearts perched in white, spray-painted nests in the center of each table.

"I'll say you did. The place looks great."

Tucker slammed the cabinet door and within seconds had the tap connected and foam flowing from the spout. Spicy ale scented the kitchen as he worked to adjust the flow from froth to rich amber, letting his latest recipe fill a plastic cup. Once satisfied, he poured a fresh pint for Travis and handed it through the window.

"On the house."

"Damn right it's on the house. Do you know how many times I climbed that ladder today?"

"Too many to count?"

"You got it." Travis tipped the plastic cup to his lips and took a healthy drink, leaving a foamy moustache above his lip. "Damned good. Just the right amount of hops."

"Thank you. I think I'll call it Raging Reindeer. It's too late to bottle it in time for the holidays, but I'll definitely make sure to have it ready for next year."

Tucker was proud of the success of his micro-brew business, Misty Mountain Brewery, which he owned with Brody. Profits had tripled since their last expansion and it was time to pursue his next endeavor—an authentic British pub. The old castle at the end of Main Street was the perfect location. He wished he could show Travis the drawings of the renovations for the building. Travis was a jack of all trades who could build or fix anything, and had a keen eye for detail. But Tucker had decided from the get-go he would keep his plans to himself and wait to see the surprise on his friends' faces when he announced his new solo venture.

"Hey, you." The back door opened with a creak and Liza came in, causing his heart to skip a beat. "What's going on?"

She draped her jacket on a hook inside the door, kicked the door closed, and flicked her long, blue hair over her shoulder. Her red T-shirt, emblazoned with *Deck the What?*, let the world know she didn't like Christmas. She hated everything about it—the lights, the music, the movies—all because of a few mishaps and one big disaster she'd had this time of year. He, on the other hand, loved every last tradition—decorating the tree, singing Christmas carols, the mistletoe. As much as he relished the season, he'd made the right decision turning down the role of Santa.

Liza came into the kitchen, drawing in a loud breath. "Tucker. Oh my God, look at you."

He shoved his slim-cut plaid shirt into his jeans and readjusted his rolled-up cuffs.

"What happened to you?" Liza patted him on the belly and he reflexively tightened his abs. "You're like a rock. Do you see this, Travis?"

"He should be in one of those Sexiest Man Alive magazines."

"Wow, thanks, man." He backhanded Travis's shoulder for such a stupid suggestion, causing beer to slop on the floor.

"Shit. Now I've got to find a mop." Travis lumbered away, shaking his wet hand between sips from the plastic cup.

"Travis is right. In fact, you could be on the cover. What've you been doing?"

His cheeks grew warm and his heart swelled. He'd never had the kind of body worth admiring and it was a little embarrassing. For the past several months, he'd been cutting back on carbs—except for beer—and had given up deep fried food. His weight loss had been slow and steady until a few weeks ago when he started working out with Derek three mornings a week. Now that he'd ditched is his old, baggy clothes, she finalized noticed.

"Just watching what I eat and working out a little. You knew I was losing weight."

"Yeah, but you've been working out more than a little. You look great. Turn around." He chuckled and threw his arms out, spinning around so she could examine the change.

"Well? You like what you see?" He rotated with a wry grin, proud his hard work had paid off. Maybe now she'd look at him differently and think of him as more than just a buddy.

"You better believe it. You're totally hot." Liza stretched up on her toes and brushed the back of her hand across his clean-shaven cheek. "No beard. And your hair is styled. What's going on, Tucker?"

Liza stepped back, perched her fists on her hips, and cocked her head to the side, studying Tucker as if he were a bug under a microscope. Her blue hair glowed under the fluorescent lights. It took guts to dye her hair in every color of the rainbow, but her free spirit was something he'd always loved about her.

"Start talking. Who is she?"

"Nah, it's nothing. Just needed to lose some weight, that's all."

"Lose some weight? One day you're a big, huggable teddy bear and the next," Liza threw out an imaginary handful of confetti. "Poof, you're a studly GQ model."

"I think that's a little over the top." Heat rose in his face. Damned if she wasn't making him blush. "The teddy bear is still in here, minus the beer belly and shaggy beard, but still very huggable."

"Well, I don't know what to say. I'm proud of you."

Liza reached up and he gathered her in his arms, lifting her off her feet. He'd known her his whole life and been in love with her almost as long. His last year of college, while home on break, he had been struck by Cupid's arrow when he'd showed up at Liza's sixteenth birthday party and discovered Brody's little sister was no longer the annoying tomboy who had always followed them around. She had grown up into a curvy, sharp-tongued, edgy, and downright sexy young woman. He had bided his time until she finished college and they both had returned to Highland Springs, hoping one day to get his chance. Spending so much time with her in the last year had deepened his love for her. If only she felt the same for him.

Liza wrapped her hands around his biceps once he lowered her to the floor. "Feel that. Your arms are like tree limbs. It's too bad you're letting this go to waste." Liza dropped her hands and poked him in the chest.

"What do you mean?"

"You should be dating someone."

"I'm too busy hanging out with you." He hoped she didn't detect the nerves in his chuckle. She was the only woman he wanted to spend time with.

"You might not want to after I tell you what I did."

"What?"

"Tucker Callum!" Virginia McNamara pushed through the swinging doors and shuffled into the kitchen. For an eighty-year-old, Kate's grandmother moved as fast as a woman half her age. "You just made my night."

"I did?"

"I'm so glad you changed your mind, honey."

"Changed my mind about what?"

"About being Mr. Claus, silly. Liza called me today to tell me. The whole committee is ecstatic."

A shooting pain swelled in his elbow where Liza's fingers dug deeply into his flesh. What the hell had she done?

"Yeah, I knew Tucker was busy today, but thought the committee should know he changed his mind. He's really excited about it, aren't you Tucker?"

He pulled his elbow out of Liza's tiger claw grip and rubbed some feeling back into his arm, giving her a *you have some explaining to do* glare. But her big, pleading blue eyes stirred a warm quiver in his belly.

"Oh, right, yes, very excited."

"Who have you picked to be Mrs. Claus?"

"It's a surprise." Liza smiled sweetly at Tucker. Her smile still melted his heart even though he could wring her neck.

"You can't keep us in suspense too long, honey. We have to announce it this evening."

"I have someone in mind. Don't worry, Virginia."

"Wonderful." Virginia laid her soft, wrinkled hand on Tucker's arm and gave it a tender squeeze. "I'm just thrilled, honey. Thank you. You'll make a wonderful Santa."

"My pleasure."

Virginia hummed "Jingle Bells" as she pushed through the swinging doors. Tucker turned around to face the little minx who had tricked him into being Mr. Claus.

"Start talking."

He lumbered closer to Liza, feigning anger while suppressing a smile. He forced her against the countertop where he hovered over her, in his most menacing guise, fighting to keep a straight face. She had just given him the opening he'd been looking for.

"I knew how much you really wanted to be Santa, so I called Virginia. You can't let this opportunity slip away. You'll make the best Mr. Claus the town has ever seen."

"Is that right?"

"The absolute best. Now don't be mad at me. You said you have someone in mind, right? Is she here tonight?"

Tucker grabbed her shoulders and glared into her beautiful, wide-eyed face. Little did she know, she had just done him a favor. She would be Mrs. Claus and they would spend the next month together, and hopefully she would give him a second chance.

"I'm not mad. Don't look so scared."

"You're not mad?"

"Nope, in fact, I'm glad you called Virginia. I really did want to be Mr. Claus."

"Oh," she sighed with relief and smiled up at him. "I'm so happy. I thought you would kill me."

"Not at all. But why'd you call her?"

"Because you'll make a really great Mr. Claus."

"I doubt that's all there is to it. But, yeah, I'm glad. It'll make this Christmas even more special."

"Christmas? Special? You mean the time of year when an asteroid is likely to strike my house?"

Tucker tossed his head back with a laugh, giving her tiny shoulders a squeeze, hoping she wouldn't slap him.

"Christmas will be extra special this year because *you* will play Mrs. Claus."

"Me?" Liza snapped out of his hold as if she'd been punched. "No way. You couldn't pay me to dress up in that goofy red dress and gray wig. Christmas is not my thing."

"You don't have to wear the costume everywhere."

"I don't want to wear it at all."

"Aw, come on. It'll be fun. Besides, you were the one who got me into this."

"Nope, not doing it. If I do, something tragic will happen. Bad luck tends to follow me around this time of year."

"Well, then, I'll just tell the committee I can't. Let someone else do it."

Tucker walked toward the swinging doors that led into the activity room. He should have known Liza wouldn't do it. Several willing women had approached him when they had heard he'd been nominated, but there was no one else he wanted by his side. Just as he pushed open the door, her firm hand cut off the circulation in his arm.

"Wait. You can't quit. You have to do it." Her eyes bulged wildly like a cornered animal. "You have to be Santa. I'll help you find someone."

"I don't have to do anything."

"Yes, you do because I told everyone at Thanksgiving dinner yesterday that you were going to do it and already had a missus picked out."

"I thought there was more to your little scheme. Why'd you tell them that?"

She released his arm and averted her gaze as she mumbled her excuse. "Because my snobby cousin Diana wants to do it and she'll make an already annoying holiday even more unbearable."

"So you threw me under the bus?"

Her head popped up and a mischievous smile spread across her face. "I'll work my matchmaking magic and find someone for you tonight."

"Forget it." He pushed past her, back into the kitchen, and picked up a lime and a long, sharp butcher knife. Liza followed close behind, but stopped short when he hacked the fruit in half.

"Tucker, you have to help me. I can't let Diana know I was making that stuff up last night. She'll never let me live it down."

"It would serve you right."

Keeping his focus on the cutting board, he sliced the lime into thin, half-moons and tossed them into a bowl. He would never understand what it was about Diana that got under Liza's skin. She wasn't half the woman Liza was. Sure, she was pretty, in a glamorous, too-much-make-up sort of way, but Liza was beautiful. She was smart, witty, and with her ever-changing hair color, she was way cooler than Diana. Holding the knife like a saber, he turned toward Liza who was nervously ringing hers hands.

"Hey, Tuck," Derek shouted through the back door. "Help us with the ice and soda, will you?"

Just when he was about to give Liza a well-deserved tongue lashing, Derek and Brody showed up. He dropped the knife on the cutting board, wiped his wet, sticky hands on a towel and brushed past her. By playing Mr. and Mrs. Claus, he had hoped to show her what an amazing person she was, convince her Christmas wasn't such a bad time of year, and ultimately win her heart. Instead, she wanted to fix him up with someone else. Maybe he should let her. Obviously, he was wasting his time on Liza.

THREE

While the men carried in supplies, Liza walked over to the bid table to see which women were signed up for the auction. Tucker could bid on one of the participants and make her Mrs. Claus, saving Liza from humiliation. Once he was finished helping Derek and Brody, she would convince him this was the best course of action. Making her Mrs. Claus would just be a recipe for disaster. A burning sensation coursed through her chest as she looked over the bid sheets.

"Thinking of bidding on someone?" Riley, her best friend, had snuck up on her and caused her pained heart to go into arrhythmia.

Liza placed a palm on her chest. "You scared the crap out of me."

"Well, are you?" Riley smirked, flipping her long, red hair over one shoulder.

"Hardly. I'm checking to see who's on the auction block that Tucker might be interested in."

"Why?"

"He needs a Mrs. Claus."

"I thought he wasn't doing it." Riley furrowed her brows as she glanced over Liza's shoulder at the list of available bachelorettes.

"He will after I pick out someone for him. But look, there are only two women who are *maybe* bid-worthy." Liza picked up the clipboard to scan the names again. "None of these others are Tucker's type or would do as Mrs. Claus." She set the list down, and shook her head.

Riley rested her hip against the table and crossed her arms. "Why do you care? I thought you hated Christmas."

"Hate is a strong word."

"Okay, you dislike Christmas."

"Can you blame me? I've told you about the stuff that's happened this time of year."

"I don't think your Barbie Dream House getting crushed by a falling Christmas tree has anything to do with Christmas per se, do you?"

"The roof crashed through to the first floor." Liza clapped her right hand down hard on top of her left. She would never forget the sound of the roof collapsing. Her holiday was ruined. "What about the year I studied abroad in Paris and I got stranded during my layover at Heathrow due to a freak blizzard? I had to sleep in the airport through Christmas day."

"Okay, that was bad, but you realize it has nothing to do with—"

"And remember the guy I dated in college sophomore year who broke up with me nine days before Christmas because he had heard that that was the latest you could break up with someone before the holidays? He ruined my winter break."

"What a creep."

"*And* I got food poisoning from the eggnog they served at the Winter Street Fest last year. I missed Beautiful Blooms' holiday open house."

"Yeah, that was awful. Several people suffered from it. I think that vendor is banned from the street fest this year."

"And let's not forget my wreck."

Liza rubbed her hand over her upper thigh and, in a flash, it all came back to her. Waking from a coma Christmas morning in the hospital, her mom slumped in a chair, sound asleep, and Liza unable to speak because of the tube down her throat. Memories of surgeries, traction, and weeks of rehab would never leave her. The last thing she remembered before waking up was Bret's cutting words, humiliating her in front of his friends. Everything else—the icy roads, extracting her body from the car using the Jaws of Life, her totaled car—had been filled in by her family.

"Okay, I get it. You've had terrible luck this time of year, but what does that have to do with who Tucker and—"

"He needs help, okay?"

"I doubt he needs help getting a date. Have you seen him?"

His diet and work-out regiment had definitely paid off. He was no longer big, dumpy Tucker, but hot, built Tucker who could have his pick of the ladies. Liza pressed her fist into the fire burning beneath her diaphragm as she glanced over the bid sheets.

"Look, my cousin, Diana, and her boyfriend threatened to go to the committee to volunteer to be Mr. and Mrs. Claus. There's no way Barbie and Ken are going to have the honors. I said Tucker was going to do it and would announce who Mrs. Claus was going to be tonight. I have to help him find someone—and fast—before Diana throws this all back in my face."

"Why don't you do it?"

"Play Mrs. Claus?" Riley had clearly lost her mind. "Didn't we just go over the fact that I really dislike this time of year?"

"But you'd help out Tucker."

"He asked me, but I said no. Believe me, something would go wrong. There has to be someone here tonight he could ask."

As they walked back toward the bar where Liza would work all evening, she surveyed the room, trying to figure out who would be a suitable Mrs. Claus.

"I don't think I've met Diana." Riley stopped in front of the old cafeteria window that now acted as a bar. Liza went inside and leaned her elbows on the shiny, stainless steel counter-top across from her.

"Trust me, you won't want to meet her. She's going out with Bret Bridges now. He was sort of nice to me last night, but I don't know why." Liza opened a sleeve of cups and stacked them one-by-one into neat, red towers beside the tap. "I've told you how my mom and Aunt Linda always forced Diana and me together growing up, even dressed us in the same clothes, like we were twins. They'd put us in little frilly dresses and

Diana's would stay pristine all day but I'd spill red Kool-Aid on mine within minutes. She just annoys me, okay?"

"I have a feeling you spilled the Kool-Aid on purpose."

"Maybe." They shared a conspiratorial smirk. Maybe subconsciously she *had* ruined their matching outfits so her mother was forced to change her into something different. She'd never really considered it before. She just figured she was the klutz and Diana was the graceful one. Even the night of the wreck, Diana had managed to escape with only a bump on the head and a broken wrist.

"They're moving back to Highland Springs, so now I'll have to see their perfection all the time." Liza rolled her eyes.

"I can't wait to meet them." Riley's smile couldn't hide the sarcasm.

Like a magnet to steel, Liza's gaze shifted toward the entryway where Diana and Bret stood, dressed like the cover of a holiday catalog. "Now's your chance. There they are."

Diana's deep brunette hair was pulled back in a classic chignon and she wore a red dress with white faux fur around the neckline. At least Bret wasn't dressed like Santa with a long red coat and wide black belt, but he was close enough. He wore black corduroy pants and a red pull-over. They were so determined to take on the roles, they even dressed the part.

"I better give some suggestions to Tucker before those two talk to the committee. Over my dead body will they be Mr. and Mrs. Claus."

She looked past Riley at the sudden influx of people filing into the activity room. The auction would soon be under way, beginning with a thirty-minute meet and mingle period. A long queue was forming in front of the window, leaving her no time to worry about Tucker. While she poured a foamy pint of beer and waited for payment, she scanned the room. She found Tucker surrounded by Kacy, Holli, and Mandy, who were all up for auction. Surely he wouldn't pay good money for a date with any of them. They were definitely not Mrs. Claus material.

Her chest burned again, like it had a few minutes ago. She had to lay off the spicy food for a few days. She kept her eyes on the beer tap and wine bottles, and not the three women vying for Tucker's attention. Any of them as Mrs. Claus made her indigestion flare—there had to be a better option. She glanced toward him as she handed a glass of wine through the window. Kacy was dragging her long nails down his sleeve. When his shoulders pumped up and down with laughter, the nagging burn in her chest became a hot fire poker. Holli laid her hand at the small of his back and Liza pressed her fist between her breasts to help ease the pain.

Tucker looked so different from the guy everyone knew. His wide, muscular shoulders tapered down to a trim waist and his new jeans accentuated his firm butt. He'd been so rough and dumpy for so long, even Liza hadn't realized such a hot guy had been hiding beneath the scruff. He sounded and acted like himself, but had been replaced by an Adonis in blue jeans. He was too good for any of those women. Between his successful business, his great personality, and his new, too-hot-for-Highland-Springs body, he had risen to Most Eligible Bachelor status and would have every single lady in the county after him. She would just have to protect him from the hungry pack of she-wolves before he made a mistake.

***

"Interviewing the future Mrs. Claus?" Liza slammed a roll of plastic cups on the metal table, causing several heads to turn as Tucker entered the kitchen. He had only left her alone for a few minutes, so why was she in such a foul mood? He hadn't totally shirked his bartending duties.

"No, just talking. Sorry I wasn't here for the early rush."

"I handled it." She brushed past him and picked up a case of red wine.

"Here, let me get that." When he took the box out of her hands, she settled her fists on her hips and scowled at him.

"What's wrong?"

"Honestly, since you got all buff and everything, you're too hot for any of those women."

Tucker chuckled as he put the wine on the counter and pulled a bottle out of the box. "What are you talking about?"

"None of them is worthy of being Mrs. Claus. You can't bid on them."

"Who said I was going to bid on them?"

"They were certainly doing all they could to get your attention."

"So?"

"So..."

"Lizard. There you are." Liza spun around so quick she stumbled against Tucker, nearly knocking the wine bottle from his hands. He set it on the counter and gripped her shoulders as Diana shuffled toward the bar with her arms outstretched and nails wiggling. Bret Bridges was a few paces behind her with a plastic grin glued to his face. Man, he hated that guy.

"What are you two doing here?" Liza backed into him and he pulled her in tight against his chest as he whispered in her ear.

"What *are* those two doing together?"

"They're dating." When she turned her head to whisper her response, bringing her mouth within kissing distance, it took all he had not to lay one on her. If only he could.

Diana cackled like a hen as she reached her arm around Bret and snuggled against his shoulder. "We thought we'd stop by, say hello to old friends, let them know we're back." Diana glanced into the kitchen. "Bartending tonight?"

"Yup. Tucker and me."

"Tucker Callum? I would've never recognized you. You look completely different." Diana batted her eyes at Tucker. "Is it the stress of running your own business?" She leaned through the window, her face drawn with feigned concern.

"The stress of—?"

"It's okay. So often folks start a new business thinking they would make a mint, but they work too many hours for too little reward. I see it all the time in the bank. Folks come in distraught because they bit off more than they could chew and they just wither away to nothing."

Liza drew in a sharp breath and her shoulders became hard as stone. When she took a step toward Diana, he pulled her back and rubbed his hands up and down her arms, settling his little pit bull. One thing he could always count on was that Liza had his back.

"And they pour their hearts out to you, don't they?" Tucker smiled warmly, playing along with Diana but fighting back a laugh. She was way off base. Misty Mountain was doing exceptionally well. After the New Year, he planned to start on the next phase of his business and looked forward to the surprise on her face when the city announced his winning bid for the castle.

Liza wiggled out of his grip and reached for a plastic cup. "So, what can we get you?" she snapped.

"White wine for me. And Bret will have a beer."

Liza scooted the beer and wine toward the edge of the bar and collected payment while Tucker leaned against a stainless steel table, studying Diana and Bret. Diana had always bugged Liza and he could understand why. She carried the same superior air toward Liza that he had always felt from Bret. Tucker had grown up in Paula's Creek where most folks had worked in the local coal mine once owned by Bret's granddaddy. When his granddaddy died, his father shut down the mine and put everyone—including Tucker's dad—out of work. It didn't matter that Bret was a few years younger than Tucker, he still treated him and anyone else from that area like dirt under his shoe. He was nothing but a spoiled, privileged asshole who Tucker blamed for Liza's wreck.

Diana sipped her wine, scowled at the cup, then regarded Liza with a raised brow. "Oh, listen, Lizard—"

"Liza." Wrapping an arm around Liza's shoulder, he wordlessly warned Diana he would stand up for his girl. "It's Liza."

"Liza…remember my offer last night? You know, about the Christmas season?" Diana gestured at Liza with her wine.

"I don't know what you're talking about." Liza moved out of Tucker's arm, picked up a cloth and began wiping down the countertop.

"You know." Through gritted teeth, Diana shot a quick glance at Tucker and leaned through the window toward Liza. "About Bret and me being Mr. and Mrs. Claus." Did she think by lowering her voice he wouldn't hear?

"Oh, yeah, about that." Tucker drew himself to his full six-foot-two height and stepped closer to the window. "Liza said you were thinking about approaching the committee to volunteer your services."

"Well, it's just, um, we—" Diana sputtered.

"Maybe next year." Tucker crossed his arms and glared at her in silent warning.

"Mr. and Mrs. Claus are usually a couple, a committed couple." Bret broke his silence and draped his arm over Diana's shoulder to emphasize their relationship.

"Well now, Bret, what makes you think I'm not committed to someone?"

"Diana's mom said you weren't dating anyone."

"Last I checked, Diana's mom doesn't know anything about my personal life."

"We just wouldn't want the people of Highland Springs to be disappointed," Diana said, coming to Bret's defense.

Tucker's hand slid around Liza's waist and he bent down, pressing his cheek to hers. "We're not going to disappoint anyone, are we, sweetheart?"

"Ah…" Liza's swallowed deep and loud.

"See, guys, you don't have anything to worry about. Liza and I will be the best Mr. and Mrs. Claus this town has ever seen."

Diana and Bret were stunned into silence, their jaws agape, carbon copies of each other.

"So, just let Virginia know you'll take over next year. But this year, it's me and my girl."

They turned quick and walked off with a huff. As soon as they were out of ear-shot, Liza turned on him, fire in her blue eyes.

"What was that all about?" Her flushed cheeks signaled she was boiling mad or embarrassed—either way, he was about to get an earful, and damned if she wouldn't be cute doing it.

"What do you mean?" He gathered the empty wine bottles cluttering the countertop and carried them toward the recycling bin. Her toe brushed the back of his heels as she trailed behind him.

"That…that…sweetheart business. *My girl* business."

He dropped the bottles in the plastic bin and turned around to begin his preemptive strike against her tongue lashing.

"You were the one who told them I would be Santa and that I had found Mrs. Claus. I didn't want to make a liar out of you, and this was your idea."

Liza's flush turned waxy. She wrung her hands, twisting them nervously. The determined gleam in her eye was replaced by fear. "But I was going to help you find someone tonight."

"I don't want anyone else to do it but you." *You, you're the only one I want—have ever wanted.*

"You know I don't like Christmas. Even if I liked Christmas, it doesn't like me."

"It'll be okay. I'm not worried."

She narrowed her eyes at him. "What was that sweetheart business a minute ago?"

He gathered her cherub face in his hands. "Bret said it had to be a real couple. I was just making it look convincing."

"Yeah, but what if—"

"Just leave it to me. We can pull this off." He placed his hands on her shoulders and squatted down to her eye level, walking her backward until she came to a halt against the walk-in refrigerator. Her eyes were as big as moons and her chest rose and fell with shallow breaths. What would she do if he placed a long, slow kiss on her quivering lips right now?

"Seriously, Tucker? How can we pull this off? When people date they—"

"Hold hands, hug, kiss? We already do that, remember?"

"But not like *that*. We hug and kiss like siblings, not lovers."

He stood up straight and laughed. "Good God, how much PDA do you expect us to do? Even if we were seriously dating, I wouldn't stick my tongue down your throat in public."

"I know, but—" She wrenched out of his hold and turned her attention to the overflowing trashcan. She twisted the ends of the plastic bag and attempted to lift it out of the barrel. "When people are dating and presumably in love, they get a certain look in their eyes, a certain expression. You know what I mean?"

"You did theatre in high school and I was quite a bullshitter in my day. We can fake it."

He grabbed the bag and pulled it free with little effort. She crossed her arms over her chest.

"But, it's my entire family we have to convince, not just Diana and Bret. This is a bad idea."

"We can tell Brody and Kate the truth, and your parents if you want." He lumbered toward the back door, carrying two enormous bags of trash in each hand. "Besides, now that I'm in shape, it only makes sense you'd date a hot guy like me." He tossed her a playful wink before he stepped into the cold night. There was no way he'd let her out of this.

FOUR

Tucker stood on Liza's porch, drawing his shoulders forward, marching in place as he blew warm air into his cupped hands. She lived in her grandparent's old house, and Brody and Kate lived in the family farmhouse at the end of the lane. He loved this place where he'd spent so much of his childhood playing with Brody and now cultivating grain on his farm for their brew-making business.

Even on this cloudy, cold morning, the view of fenced dormant fields and the river and mountains in the distance reminded him of a Currier and Ives painting. The ribbon of smoke coming from the old farmhouse chimney added to the idyllic scene. His heart warmed even more when Liza threw open her front door.

"What are you doing here?"

Not the greeting he'd been dreaming of, but she still looked damned cute in her ripped jeans and leather boots. Clouds like thin cotton came out of his mouth as he spoke.

"Picking you up for brunch."

She grabbed hold of his arm and tugged him into her foyer. "Get in here. You'll freeze to death out there."

They were headed to Brody and Kate's for their monthly Sunday brunch where everyone would gather around the dining room table, chat about the holidays, and make a fuss over their baby, John Brody. Tucker's pick for Mrs. Claus was bound to be a topic of discussion.

"You didn't need to pick me up. I usually walk over by myself."

He shrugged out of his coat and followed her into the kitchen. "I just thought since we're a couple now, we should be—"

"Whoa. Hold on there, mister." She stopped so fast he slammed into her. "We're faking remember?" She spun like a top and planted her hands on her hips.

"Of course. But I wasn't sure if your aunt and uncle or Diana and Bret would be at brunch today and thought it would look more legit if we arrived together."

Liza considered him for a moment. "Good thinking. You're right."

Gusting winds tossed the pines back and forth through the little window above the kitchen sink. It rattled the back storm door and sent a cold shiver down Tucker's back. It was a frigid, gray morning. They could ride over in his warm truck, but the image of Liza snuggled against him as they walked down the lane, arms around each other, her wind-tossed hair tickling his face, heated him in all the right places.

"The more we're seen together, the more convincing we'll be," he said, fighting to keep the grin off his face.

"Okay, then. Since you roped me into this—"

"Who roped who?"

"—from now until the Mistletoe Ball, I will do my best performance of a smitten girlfriend in red velvet and fur."

"You'll be the best Mrs. Claus Highland Springs has ever seen."

"Don't say that." She waved her arms as if to ward off the evil spirits. "You'll jinx it. The less you say and the more we fly under the radar, the better the chance nothing awful will happen."

"Fine. No more mention of Christmas. Let's go. I'm starved."

Tucker left his truck in her driveway and they walked down the gravel lane, her arm looped through his as they huddled against the biting wind. As they crested the knoll, they were met with an enthusiastic howl from Loretta, Brody's German shorthaired pointer. She charged toward them with a graceful gallop and dove into Tucker's outstretched arms. No one had told Loretta she was no longer a little puppy, but fifty pounds of solid muscle.

"How's my girl?" He hefted the dog on his shoulder and gave her a hearty pat on the back. "Ready for our hunting trip?"

"I don't know who loves deer hunting more—you guys or Loretta."

"Definitely Loretta. She doesn't mind the cold."

He lowered the dog to the ground and she ran ahead, barking out the news that they had arrived. "So how are we going to play this?" He followed Loretta's brown speckled body up the porch steps, Liza on his heels.

"What do you mean?"

Stopping at the front door, Tucker thumbed toward the driveway. "Looks like your aunt and uncle's car. We have to act like a real couple."

"Okay, how about—"

"There you are." Liza's mom opened the door, holding Kate and Brody's baby swaddled tight against her chest. Since she and Tucker hadn't had time to prepare their act, they'd just have to wing it.

Once they were inside and had shed their coats, Liza lifted the corner of the blanket draped over her nephew and pecked a light kiss on his dark, fuzzy head. "How's my baby?" she murmured against his scalp, drawing in a deep breath of him. J.B. cooed against his grandmother's shoulder, and then lifted his face toward Liza.

"Look at you, big man. So strong." She tweaked the baby's cheek and smiled lovingly at the blue bundle. Tucker's chest clenched. This was what he wanted, the American dream: a house, two point five kids, a dog, and he wanted it all with Liza.

"Hand him over, Mom. I want to hold him." Sherri reluctantly handed J.B. to Liza, patting the baby's back while Liza settled him against her shoulder.

"Look, Tucker." Liza tilted J.B. out for Tucker to see. One pink fist was pressed against his mouth while his dark eyes shifted toward the voices coming from the kitchen. "Isn't he beautiful?"

He agreed John Brody was a beautiful baby and Liza was a natural with him. Could they have such a future? He had to tread lightly during the next month if he was going to win her heart. She continuously reminded him they were only friends, rejecting him once before.

"Do you want to hold him?"

She didn't give him a chance to answer. She pushed the baby into his arms who immediately let out a blood-boiling scream. Undeterred by J.B.'s outburst, Tucker placed a hand at the baby's bottom and one behind his head and bobbed him up and down while giving him a talk.

"Now, listen up, little buddy. This is no way to treat your Uncle Tucker." Still bouncing, he strolled down the hallway toward the living room, looking J.B. in the eye. "We're going to take a little walk and get things settled between us."

"Don't bounce him too hard." Liza shadowed them down the hall, chirping out instructions. "Keep your hand behind his head. Make sure his blanket stays tucked."

"Aunt Liza doesn't think I know what I'm doing," Tucker said to the baby. "She forgets I've got four nieces and nephews." He chuckled, imagining holding their own baby as Liza barked out instructions.

John Brody shoved his fist in his mouth, reducing his cries to whimpers. "Thanks, bud. I appreciate you working with me here."

Now that the baby had settled down, Tucker gathered him into the crook of his arm and took him over to the half-decorated Christmas tree. J.B.'s eyes dodged left and right, taking in the bright white lights twinkling among the branches. His sweet new-baby smell made Tucker's insides go soft. Liza sidled up to him and rested her hand against his back while she tickled the baby's cheek.

"He's really watching the lights, isn't he?" Her breast pressed into Tucker's arm as she rubbed J.B.'s earlobe between her fingers. He inhaled her soft cologne while fighting the urge to wrap his arm around her.

"You'll have to put up a tree this year. J.B. will love it." He leaned into her, brushing the top of her head with his chin. "Now that you're an aunt, you can't boycott Christmas anymore."

"Just watch me." Her big, blue eyes gave him a warning glare.

"Well, who do we have here?" Liza's Aunt Linda screeched from across the room. "Is this the Christmas couple?"

Tucker winked at Liza, whose face screwed up in a scowl. She should have known the news would spread fast. Ready or not, their performance was about to begin. He wrapped his arm around her shoulder and turned the three of them around to face her aunt who came to an abrupt halt.

"Tucker Callum?" Linda's mouth hung open, her eyes darting between the two of them. "Look at you. You're like a different person."

His cheeks grew warm, still not quite comfortable with all the attention from his weight loss. Six months ago, staring at Liza while Brody and Kate exchanged their vows, he had decided he wouldn't follow in the footsteps of the men his family. His father and uncles had all died of heart attacks before the age of fifty. He wanted to live a long, full life, and wanted to live it with Liza. Hoping for a future with her only strengthened his determination to get in shape.

Tucker plastered a smile on his face. "Hello, Mrs. Murray."

"Hi, Aunt Linda. Tucker looks great, doesn't he?" Liza pecked a quick kiss on her aunt's cheek and dug her nails into Tucker's elbow, forcing him to follow her into the kitchen. He chuckled against the baby's head as they left Linda gaping after them.

"Oh, my God. Why did she have to be here?" Liza whispered as they entered the kitchen.

"It's show time," Tucker said in his best master of ceremony voice.

"We're not ready. We should've practiced."

"Did you all know Liza was dating Tucker?" Aunt Linda had stealthily followed them into the kitchen where Liza's dad, Brody, and Kate sat at the kitchen table. Startled by the screeching outburst, Kate's grandmother dropped the spatula she was using to fry sausage.

"My gracious, you nearly stopped this old girl's heart." Virginia pressed her hand against her chest as she bent to retrieve the spatula from the floor. "I'm eighty years old. You can't sneak up on me like that."

"I'm sorry, Virginia, but I wasn't aware Liza had a new boyfriend. Mr. Claus, no less."

"New boyfriend? They've been dating for lord knows how long." Virginia winked at Liza and Tucker before systematically flipping each sausage in the pan. Liza's mouth hung open and he, too, wondered how Virginia knew to play along. Looking at the threesome around the table, Tucker found the same look of surprise. Their eyes shifted between one another signaling that they hadn't heard the news.

"How did I not know about this? Why didn't you tell us at Thanksgiving?" Linda looked stricken that she'd been left out of the loop.

"If you'd come down off that mountain every once in a while, you'd know what's going on in town." Virginia threw out her quip, never taking her eyes off the sausage.

"Well, excuse me." Linda pulled out a chair and plopped into it with a huff. "I guess some people are privy to news and some aren't." She crossed her arms over her chest, pouting like a spoiled child. "You could've told us at Thanksgiving instead of being so cryptic."

A loud crash came from outside the back door, ending her aunt's protests and rattling the windows. Brody rushed to the back door. "A pine tree just fell in the driveway."

"Oh, no, it's starting." Liza flopped into a kitchen chair and covered her face with her hands.

"Almost hit your truck, Dad," Brody said, looking through the door's glass.

"Well, I'll be damned." Doug joined Brody at the back door, scratching his head at the scene out back.

"The curse is striking my family now." Liza moaned her lament into her hands. "Why does this keep happening?"

"There is no curse and his truck wasn't damaged. You've got to stop this." Tucker shoved J.B. back in Liza's arms and followed Brody, Rodney, and Doug outside. The men circled the tree, surveying the situation and commenting on its source. One thing was for sure—a curse didn't cause the tree to fall. If it had, the tree would have landed on top of her dad's truck, not six inches from the front bumper.

"I guess with the wind and all the rain we've had that old tree didn't stand a chance," Doug said as he jumped into his vehicle and backed it away several feet. It took all four men to shove the tree flat onto the driveway.

"Hey, Tuck, can you give me a hand?" Brody waved Tucker toward the shed where he stored tools. "We'll cut this up and have it out of the way in a few minutes."

Once inside the cool, dark shed, Brody turned on Tucker. "What the hell's going on in there? What's this about you two dating?"

Tucker shrugged. "We're this year's Mr. and Mrs. Claus."

"What the hell?" His confusion turned to shock.

"Liza told me about what happened at Thanksgiving, about her telling everyone I was going to be Santa, and I offered to cover for her. In return, she will be Mrs. Claus." Tucker grinned at his luck. He'd waited years for an opportunity like this.

"She agreed to that? Everyone knows she hates Christmas." Brody said.

"Yeah, well…"

"You'll never pull this off. Diana and Bret will see right through her." Brody stalked to the back of the shed and hoisted the chainsaw in his hand. "Trying to one-up Diana will blow up in Liza's face."

"She just doesn't want them to be the Christmas couple and now needs to save face. Besides, anything to stick it to Bret Bridges is okay with me." He picked up an ax and a hand saw, and walked out the door. "I wasn't going to be Mr. Claus, but since Liza needs my help, I figured why not?"

"Well, good luck. I hope you won't regret this."

Tucker slapped a hand on Brody's shoulder with a loud laugh. "Oh, it'll probably come back to bite me."

FIVE

The back door swung open, and Tucker and Brody stomped their way into the laundry room. Cold air filtered into the kitchen where Liza was scooping scrambled eggs into a large bowl and Kate was retrieving muffins from the oven.

"How'd it go?" Liza glanced out the kitchen window. In short order, they had cleared the tree from the driveway and stacked the logs in a neat pile.

"All clear," Brody said as he poured two cups of coffee, handing one to Tucker.

"You're just in time," Kate took off her oven mitts and tossed them on the counter. "We're ready to eat. Tucker, we saved you a place next to Liza." She winked at Liza as she took off her apron. With everyone playing along, she and Tucker just might pull this off, saving her the humiliation of Diana knowing the truth.

Tucker and Brody followed Liza and Kate into the dining room, where everyone was already seated around the table covered with heaping plates of pancakes, bacon and sausage, fruit, and pastries. The sweet and savory smells made Liza's mouth water. She had barely taken her seat when Aunt Linda started in.

"So, I want to hear all about you two. When did you start dating? Everything." Linda waved her hands in the air like an orchestra conductor before accepting the basket of muffins.

"There's not much to tell." Liza took a sip of coffee, keeping her nose tipped into the mug, drawing in its aroma as she gave herself time to come up with an explanation. The room had gone silent.

"I've known Liza since the day she was born." Tucker picked up his coffee cup and tipped it toward Linda. "That's how we met."

Liza had heard the story several times over the years. Tucker had come home from school with Brody that day and they found her mother panting and clenching her back on the porch steps. The boys, just six years old, ran the rest of the way up the gravel drive to help her. Doug was inside calling Brody's grandmother to ask if the boys could stay there while he took Sherri to the hospital to deliver a tiny baby sister.

"But when did you start dating?"

Liza rolled her eyes at Kate, who was staring at her from across the table. Couldn't Aunt Linda just let it go? Did she really need every detail of their "love story?"

"Well—" Liza needed to get Aunt Linda off this line of questioning before things got out of hand, but Tucker stepped in.

"Liza and I have been good friends for a long time. In fact, I feel like a part of this family."

The entire Fisk clan nodded in agreement.

"But last year, I had the flu and couldn't work at the brewery, and Brody was in Nashville. So, Liza stepped up and ran the tasting room and everything for me. Every day she came to check on me, even bringing me a quart of her homemade soup and buttermilk biscuits—didn't you, babe?"

Tucker wrapped an arm around her shoulder and kissed her temple. He was laying it on way too thick. Anyone who knew Liza knew she didn't make homemade soup or biscuits. In fact, her idea of cooking was macaroni and cheese from a box and a bag of pre-washed salad. Baking desserts was her only culinary talent. But from the look on Aunt Linda's face, she was totally falling for it.

"The day my fever broke, she came in and laid a crocheted blanket over me—one she'd made herself—and when I looked into her gorgeous blue eyes, I fell. I can't explain it, but I knew I was in love."

"Oh, precious." Aunt Linda swooned against the back of her chair, clasping her hands under her chin. "What a beautiful story. People just don't do like that for each other anymore."

"Oh, Aunt Linda, don't believe him. You know I can't cook or crochet." Liza swatted Tucker on the shoulder. "What really happened was—"

"It was during our wedding, right?" Kate decided to join in the storytelling. Liza glared at her, willing her to stay out of it. "You were my maid of honor and Tucker was Brody's best man. Something about the beautiful day and all the love in the air. It was contagious."

"Not exactly—" Liza once again was interrupted, this time by Brody.

"The way I remember it was Tucker and I had a meeting with a distributor in Pittsburgh. Liza wanted to visit some art galleries, so she tagged along. By the time we got to Pittsburgh, Tucker sent me to talk to the distributor alone and he and Liza went off to the galleries. During the ride back, you never would've known I was in the car. They totally ignored me. To this day, Tucker won't tell me what happened that afternoon."

"Oh, now, bud, that's our little secret." Tucker smiled and stuffed a muffin in his mouth.

"There was no little secret." Liza shook her head, pinching the bridge of her nose. The whole thing was unraveling before her eyes. They just needed to act like a couple, not fabricate a long, romantic tale. "I took Tucker to some galleries I really like because I want to open one here someday. That's it."

"That's nice, dear, but I'm confused. How did you start dating exactly?" Aunt Linda asked, bewilderment etched across her face.

"Listen, Aunt Linda—"

"I know exactly when I fell." Tucker lifted her hand and placed it in his, his brown eyes warm as he gazed into hers. "The night of her wreck. We were skating on the frozen river and I told her someday I'd be the perfect man for her. And I was right, huh, sweetheart?"

Man, he wasn't kidding when he said he had been a heck of a bullshitter in his day. He still was. He wasn't there the night of her wreck. If he had been, she would've skated away with him rather than drive home on icy roads.

"I, um…that's not exactly—"

"I guess you could say we've loved each other so long we can't pinpoint an exact time when it all began."

He draped his arm across the back of her chair, brushing his thumb against the base of her neck. When she smiled up at him, feigning happiness, the tightly clenched fork in her hand dropped to the table. Just a moment ago she wanted to stab him with it, but now his dark brown eyes were locked on hers and a warm tingle coursed to her nether regions. That was some cockamamie story, but Tucker's Oscar-worthy performance had convinced Aunt Linda. With the tenderness in his voice as he told the story and his hand rubbing her shoulder, even she was starting to believe it herself.

SIX

Business was brisk at Sit and Sip, the local version of Starbucks, with nearly every table filled. Hissing steam from the espresso machine and grinding coffee beans overlaid huddled conversations around the room. Tucker rolled his thumb over his cell phone screen as he drank from his paper cup.

"Hey, you." Liza slipped her tiny frame into the wooden chair across from him, setting her coffee cup on the table. She was loaded down with a thick accordion folder and her laptop, which she dropped on the chair beside her.

"Morning." He placed his cell phone face-down on the table and leaned back in his chair. He held his steaming cup between his hands, taking in the change of hair color—pink—which, crazy as it was, seemed to intensify her blue eyes. For the past year, they had met every Monday morning for coffee, but today it felt different, as if they were truly a couple. Yesterday at brunch he'd experienced a bit of what their future could be.

"Hello." She snapped her fingers in front of his eyes, jarring him from his musing. "Is anyone home?" She rapped her knuckle on his forehead.

"Sorry. Just thinking."

"Well, don't hurt yourself." She chuckled as she tipped her cup.

"What have you got there?"

"Oh, it's nothing." She swatted the air as if a fly were nagging her. "Just some paperwork from, uh, you know, invoices from Christmas card sales and bills."

"I thought you said you were finished with all that for the year."

"Well, you know how it is. Last minute stuff." She placed her cup on the table, and swirled it in circles, not meeting his eyes. "What about you? What've you got going today?"

"Me? Oh, just the usual. Heading out to the brewery, nothing out of the ordinary, checking on orders and such." Actually, he was headed to Charleston to meet with the architect to go over final changes to the castle renovations, and he had an appointment at a bank to discuss financing the project should he be awarded the bid. He wanted to tell her about his plans, but wanted even more to surprise her. "Want to go out to dinner tonight?"

That got her attention. "Dinner?"

"We're dating, remember? Mr. and Mrs. Claus?"

"Yes, of course. It's important to keep up appearances." Liza glanced at her watch and then consulted the calendar on her phone. "Um, sure, but can we wait until seven?"

Tucker snorted, and leaned back in the chair. "Those invoices going to keep you busy until then?"

"No, but I just have things to do."

"Yeah? Like what?"

"Just stuff, okay?" Liza fussed with her accordion folder, straightening the file, and not meeting Tucker's eyes again.

Tucker threw his hands up in surrender while his lips curled in amusement. "Now that you're Mrs. Claus, you might want to reconsider your wardrobe." She wore a red and green "Merry Whatever" T-shirt, which probably wasn't the best choice under the circumstances. "Time to stop boycotting Christmas."

"I'm not boycotting exactly." Liza lifted her cup to her lips and said over the steam, "I just don't get into all the tinsel, reindeer, Santa crap."

"Let me get this straight." He slid his coffee cup into the center of the table and rested his elbows on the edge. "You, Miss Award-Winning Watercolor Artist, who paints custom-made Christmas cards, hates Christmas. Explain to me again how that's possible?"

"It was only one award." Her eyes narrowed as she glanced away. "I haven't always hated Christmas. Besides, I'm not stupid. Those cheesy Christmas cards help pay the bills."

"Maybe as Mr. Claus, I'll help you recapture your love of the holiday." Tucker picked up his coffee.

"Don't do me any favors." She raised her hand up like a crossing guard as he chuckled against the plastic lid. "You heading to the brewery soon?"

"Trying to get rid of me?"

"No, it's just—" She rolled her eyes toward the chair and patted the thick folder. "—lots of work to do."

"I can take a hint." He stood, plunging his arms into his leather jacket while savoring one last look at her. He had to make tonight special. It could be the official start of something special—the beginning of their love story, eight years in the making. "I'll pick you up at seven."

"Pick me up? I'll meet you."

"Nope, like you said we have to keep up appearances. We're a couple out on a date, so I'm picking you up."

"Whatever you say, *Mr. Claus.*"

"That's the spirit, Mrs. Claus." Tucker dropped a kiss on Liza's cheek, leaving her with her mouth hanging open as he strolled out of the shop. With a little planning and finesse, he just might turn this charade into the real thing.

***

Tucker was carrying this ruse too far. Yesterday at brunch he spun a web of romantic lies and now he offered to take her to dinner, and left a kiss on her cheek. She laid her hand against the lingering sweetness of his gesture. Sure, they'd dined together before, and he'd even kissed her cheek, but never with such a feeling of intimacy. Surely this was all an act. He only saw her as Brody's little sister who also happened to be his friend. Taking that friendship further, especially this time of year, would only result in disaster.

"Liza."

The deep voice made her jump in her chair, causing her to plug the wrong numbers into the financial statement she was creating for her appointment at the bank later today. She lowered the lid on her laptop and shifted her gaze toward Bret, who was standing over her left shoulder.

"I'm surprised to find you here at this hour," he said, pointing at an empty chair. "May I?"

She gestured awkwardly toward the chair. What did he think the two of them could possibly talk about? He was dating her fabulous cousin—that certainly wasn't an interesting topic. Or maybe he'd rather re-hash their high school years. That could make for some uncomfortable conversation.

"I was happy to hear at Thanksgiving you're still painting." Bret adjusted his necktie and unbuttoned his navy blazer with quivering hands. Was he nervous?

"Yup, I'm still painting." She sat back in her chair and draped her leg over her knee. "I have a commissioned piece I'll start later this week."

"Commissioned? That means someone hired you to paint something for them?"

"That's what it means." She kept her gaze zeroed on him, fighting an eye roll. She had seen little of Bret since the night at the river which had ended in the wreck that had ruined Christmas for her once and for all. During those few times he'd barely spoken a word to her.

Bret nodded, and smiled. "That's impressive. Congratulations."

"You seem surprised."

"Not really. I knew you had talent. Even back in high school I recognized your artistic abilities."

Liza arched a brow in Bret's direction. "I remember those abilities helped you pass the class."

His complexion darkened as he snickered with embarrassment. "Thanks to you I got an A. You might remember I don't have an artistic bone in my body, but we had fun in that class."

"Think so?"

"Definitely. It was the best class of the semester because of you." His lips curled seductively and his eyes narrowed, but even with his handsome, classic, country-club looks, he made her skin crawl.

"Well…" She squirmed in her chair. He was so earnest and complimentary, but she didn't trust him. Her memory was sketchy, but she knew he had said some terrible things prior to her getting behind the wheel. Diana was in the car when they hit the tree, and though Liza still couldn't remember everything, she knew Diana caused the wreck. Of all her Christmas catastrophes, that was the one that stung the most.

"I was happy to hear you're still planning on opening your gallery. Honestly, as much as you talked about it in high school, I thought you would've done it by now."

"It takes time." Liza shrugged, and sipped her coffee.

"But you found a location?"

"Maybe, but I still need to do some preliminary work before I get open." And then she would create the foremost art gallery in the region, proving once and for all to her family that she could be a success. Anything Diana had accomplished would pale in comparison. "What about you? What are you into these days?"

"I'm working for my dad. I've taken over the central division."

"Running your chain of convenience stores and gas stations?"

"Right, we've just opened three more stores. Doing really well."

"Glad to hear it."

"We're looking into buying that block at the end of Main Street."

"The castle?" Now *her* hands quivered. If Bridges Enterprises bid on the property, there would be no way she could buy the building. They had too much money and power. The measly mortgage she planned to take out on her house would never compete with their millions.

"Yeah. That corner will make a great location for another gas station."

"But the castle is a historical building. My great-grandfather built it. You can't tear it down."

"It's not protected as a historical building. It may have been nice back in the 1920s, but if you ask me, it's just an eyesore."

Her stomach roiled at the thought of that beautiful, majestic stone building reduced to a pile of rubble only to be replaced with a pre-fabricated building and gas pumps.

"Can't you find another location?"

"Why would we want to?"

Because that's my gallery!

"Because it's a landmark, a legacy, a reminder to us all that some things are too important to tear down."

Liza shot out of her chair and, by the number of faces staring at her, she must have spoken too loudly. Bret rocked back in his chair, surprised by her outburst. They couldn't tear it down. They just couldn't. That was her gallery, her dream, her great-grandfather's dream. She had to find a way to convince him the corner would be a bad location for his company. One by one, folks returned to their conversations or portable devices, and her blood pressure gradually returned to normal. She settled into her seat and lifted her cup with a shaking hand.

"What would you suggest someone do with it?" Bret asked.

"They could convert it into a restaurant or a theatre or a museum. Something other than another gas station."

"Do you have any idea how much money it would take to fix that place up? It's been home to pigeons and other vermin for years. They don't call it Crap-a-Lot for nothing."

That was a nickname she'd never heard before.

"The plaster walls are crumbling, the doors are rotted. I could go on and on. The best thing we could do is set a wrecking ball to it."

"You've been inside?"

"Sure. It needs to be condemned."

That's not what she saw when Darla had taken her through the building. Yes, it had been neglected for too many years, but it was a solid building, with thick oak doors and wide ornate woodwork. The mullioned windows and turn-of-the-century light fixtures added to the historic ambiance—perfect for her gallery.

"It may need work on the inside, but the outside is solid granite. It will take more than a wrecking ball to knock it down," she said.

"I'm not sure there is much you will be able to do about it. The city is accepting bids starting next week, and I feel confident we'll get it. The town stands to gain a lot of money in tax revenue with our plan."

"No way. The committee can't award the bid to you."

"Liza." He reached across the table with a patronizing snicker. "I'm sorry, but I don't see how you or anyone else can stop it."

She snatched her arm away, his touch like a cattle prod against her skin. "Just watch me."

She gathered her laptop under her arm, slung her purse over her shoulder, and stormed off, knocking chairs with her hip and brushing by customers on her way to the door. Once outside, she drew in a lungful of cold, mountain air, trying to settle her thumping heart. That beautiful building couldn't meet with a five-ton wrecking ball. Sitting all alone on the bare lot at the end of town, the castle wasn't an eyesore at all, but a majestic medieval fortress with its two corner towers and parapet firmly rooted in the town's history. The castle *would* become her gallery, no matter what she had to do.

SEVEN

"Rack 'em up, bud." Travis flipped his long, blond dreadlocks over his shoulder and lifted his finger to signal a waitress. "This place is packed tonight."

"Friday night. What did you expect?" Tucker slowly removed the triangle from around the perfectly aligned pool balls and pointed his cue at Travis. "Break 'em."

Tucker tipped his beer toward his lips and glanced over his shoulder at the bar. With her hands above her head, Liza did a little Latin dance, shaking the cocktail shaker to the beat of the music. He chuckled as he took a long pull on his beer and watched her pour a pink concoction across three frosted martini glasses. She handed them to a group of stylish young women gathered at the bar.

"Hey, you playing or not?" Impatiently, Travis tapped his pool cue on the edge of the table. "What's got your attention over there?"

Tucker shook his head as he bent over the table, lining up a straight diagonal shot. "Nothing."

"Well, you've sure been more interested in what's going on over there than this game. Is it that group of ladies at the bar?"

"Nah. It's nothing." The white ball shot off the end of his cue like a rocket, sinking a striped ball in the pocket. He went around to the opposite end of the pool table, where he could covertly catch a glimpse of Liza at work. He had a hunch the three Cosmo drinking girls at the bar were friends of Diana's. The way they'd been watching Liza then gossiping in a huddle gave him the distinct impression they'd heard the rumors. He didn't know the group of women sidled up to the bar, but it might be worth it to check them out.

"You're on fire tonight." Travis once again signaled the waitress shuffling from one table to the next. "I don't think we're going to get a refill at this rate."

"Let me get this round." Travis had provided the perfect excuse to head to the bar. As he approached, Liza was pouring a draft beer, smiling and talking to a man sitting by the taps while the three fashion models kept up their chatter. He squeezed between them and an empty barstool, and leaned his elbow on the bar. Liza must have sensed his presence because her gaze popped up from the frothy glass and a huge smile spread across her face, melting his heart.

"Hey, you. From here it looks like you've been kicking Travis's butt."

His mouth stretched into a playful grin. "You've been checking me out?"

"Oh, yeah, I always check you out." She winked at him and gathered three beer glasses in her hands, shuffling toward the end of the bar. Out the corner of his eye, he saw the threesome gather in a tight circle, never taking their eyes off Liza.

When she returned, she planted herself directly in front of Tucker and rose onto her on tiptoes, rubbing his smooth cheek with the back of her hand. If she only knew what her friendly gesture did to him.

"What can I get you?"

"Two beers. Misty—"

"Misty Mountain. You got it."

She hustled to a set of taps on the opposite end of the bar while he rested his folded arms on the wood. When she stopped to talk with another customer, he overheard the women beside him whispering.

"I bet that's him."

"Do you think?"

"Has to be. Did you see how she winked at him and touched his cheek?"

"He doesn't look like her type at all."

Tucker's ears perked up when he realized they *were* talking about him. He reached across the bar toward the napkins, leaning close enough to notice them looking at him through his periphery.

"Yeah, he's way too hot for her."

"Maybe he thawed her out. You know what they always said about her." The threesome giggled. "I'm going to text Diana right now."

So, they *were* Diana's friends. He'd suspected it by the way they were dressed. Short skirts, high heels, and flashy jewelry weren't the usual dress code at the Brass Rail. He'd never seen them before—obviously, he and the models didn't run in the same social set.

"She's coming down. I wonder if she knows him."

"I can't believe Liza could snag a guy like that."

Tucker pushed off from the bar and worked his way to the waitress station. He flagged Liza in his direction.

"Why'd you move?" She set two foamy pints in front of him.

"Don't look, but do you know those girls clustered there in the middle of the bar?"

"Yeah, I went to high school with them."

"Well, they've figured out—"

She held up her finger. "Hold that thought. I have to take care of these guys in the corner." She rushed away before he could tell her news of their "relationship" had spread through Highland Springs.

So far, he thought it had been limited to brunch at Brody and Kate's, but he shouldn't be surprised. They lived in a small town where news spread like wildfire. He had done his part to help spread the news by taking her to dinner Monday night at his mom's diner, where gossip and eavesdropping were on the daily menu. Diana was on her way to the bar, so it was important they looked and acted like a real couple.

He picked up the beers, fighting back a grin as he returned to the pool table. He had a plan to make things more interesting.

After they finished their last pool game, he and Travis relinquished the table to a couple of oil guys and grabbed the last two seats at the end of the bar. From their vantage point, Tucker could keep an eye on the door and Diana's friends.

"Why don't you just go over and talk to them already." Travis nudged him hard, causing his beer to slop over the side of the glass onto his hand.

"I'm not—" Tucker sucked the beer off his knuckles and wiped the rest on his jeans. "I'm not checking them out. Well, I am, but not the reason you think."

"Then why is it every time I ask you a question, you don't answer because you're locked and loaded on those girls."

"They're Diana's friends, Liza's cousin."

"So?"

"So—" Just as he was about to explain the situation, the heavy, wooden door opened and Diana breezed in, waving to her posse as if the queen had arrived.

"That's Diana," he said, taking a sip of his beer.

"Oh, yeah, I've met her before. Is she the one you're interested in?"

"Just wait and see." Tucker took another fortifying gulp of his beer and strolled around the bar to the waitress station. He could feel Diana and her friends watching him as he lifted the hinged counter and stepped behind the bar. A nervous thrum went through his veins when he urged Liza over with a crook of his finger. She closed the cash register drawer and walked toward him, taking a quick order on her way.

"What's up?" She wiped her hands on a towel that he pulled from her grasp as he gathered her hands in his.

"What're you doing?" Liza's eyes bulged with surprise as he pressed his cheek against hers.

"Diana just came in," he whispered in her ear. "Don't look."

She kept a sweet smile on her face as she murmured through gritted teeth. "What the hell is she doing here?"

He pressed his lips against her hands. "Her friends called her. I overheard them talking about me. They figured out I'm your *boyfriend*."

"That big blabber mouth." If anyone was watching, they'd believe her dreamy smile was sincere, but he could see the color in her cheeks deepen. Anger was simmering just below the surface. "I bet she's spread it all over town about you and me."

"Of course, she did. Maybe we should kiss, you know, just for—"

Before he could finish his sentence, she hurled herself into his arms and pressed her lips to his. An electric buzz surged through his chest. How long had he wanted to take her in his arms and feel the softness of her mouth against his? Her body aligned with his? His heartbeat quickened when he realized she wasn't holding back; in fact, she was kissing him with unbridled enthusiasm. They stayed locked together for a moment, and when he placed her securely back on the floor, she stared up at him, her eyes as big as saucers.

"That was—"

"Weird," she said, slightly breathless.

"But—"

"Nice."

She launched herself into his arms again and crushed her lips against his. He cupped her head in the palm of one hand and wrapped his other hand around her tiny waist. She tickled his lips apart with her tongue, surprising him with a deep, passionate kiss that went way beyond anything he'd imagined. She grazed her fingertips inside the neckline of his shirt, sending a lightning bolt from the base of his neck on south. They finally tore themselves apart, panting, when the entire bar broke out in applause.

Liza pulled her hands from around his neck, her face blazing red, and smoothed the hem of her "Bah Humbug" T-shirt over the waistband of her jeans. He was sure his face was as red as hers as the applause grew into whistles and shouts.

"I guess there's no turning back now." She tipped her head into his chest, her shoulders shaking under his hands, and then threw back her head with laughter. "I've got to get back to work, *honey*." She said it loud enough for those around them to hear.

"Okay, babe." Tucker gave her bottom a gentle smack and lifted the waitress counter. He glanced over his shoulder at Liza, catching an expression he couldn't decipher. Fake or not, it appeared she had enjoyed that kiss as much as he did which was exactly what he had hoped for.

***

Liza slumped back against the refrigerator, rubbing her forehead, willing the swirling dervish inside her brain to stop spinning. They had just kissed—in front of God, Diana, and everyone else in the bar. Out the corner of her eye was a row of faces, like blackbirds on a telephone wire, watching her with interest. This ruse of theirs wasn't supposed to happen like this, not with so much realism. That kiss was way more than she expected. She liked it—more than liked it—that kiss was incredibly hot and she hadn't wanted it to stop. Everyone in the bar had seen them solidly confirm their *relationship*. Maybe playing Mr. and Mrs. Claus would be fun after all. But after the holidays they would have to come up with a reasonable break-up story. No matter how great the kiss, she couldn't risk losing his friendship.

Bleary-eyed, she glanced down the bar toward Diana and her friends, catching them staring at her. Tucker was once again seated at the end of the bar beside Travis. He gave her a killer smile and a wink, and her insides turned to jelly. He was her friend—that was all. She wasn't supposed to feel so...so...on fire. But, God help her, she liked that toe-curling kiss.

"Hey, girlfriend."

She snapped out of her reverie when Diana leaned across the counter, capturing her arm. She was surrounded by her high school friends—ones Liza had always thought of as the "mean girls." They were the cheerleaders and prom princesses—definitely a different crowd than the art club and band geeks Liza had run around with in high school.

"So..." Diana drew out the word, as if she were pulling a string of taffy from her mouth. "When were you going to tell me how serious it was with you and *Tucker Callum*?"

"What's that supposed to mean?"

"I just never thought of the two of you together. He's so much older than you."

"He's only six years older. That doesn't make him a senior citizen."

"But he's your brother's best friend." Diana's lips puckered as she passed judgment.

"So what?"

"What does Brody think about it?"

"You know what?" Liza laid her hand over Diana's, still gripping her arm. "I don't really care."

She tugged her arm out of Diana's grasp and strolled back toward the end of the bar. If her relationship with Tucker became real she wouldn't care what Brody or anyone else thought. A grin stretched across her face, knowing Diana and her friends were probably staring at her with their mouths hanging open. Between Tucker's kiss and Diana's reaction to the unlikely alliance, this little game might be fun after all.

EIGHT

Liza tossed and turned all night long, finally giving up on sleep at six o'clock. Kate would be up with John Brody, so she tugged on her boots and her down jacket, and trudged through the dark up the lane to their house. A yellow light glowed in the nursery window, confirming Liza's assumption. She climbed the steps to the back door and lifted the mat, retrieving the key from underneath. Loretta met her at the door with an eardrum-splitting bark.

"Shh, girl. It's just me."

As quietly as possible, she climbed the staircase to the baby's room.

"Oh, God." Kate jumped and J.B. let out a furious wail at the loss of his breakfast. "You scared me to death." She resettled him against her breast, stifling his protests. "There you go, baby."

"I'm sorry. I saw the light on and needed to talk to you." Liza whispered as she rubbed her hand over J.B.'s fuzzy head. "Sorry, little man."

Kate settled back in the rocking chair. "Why are you up so early? I thought you worked last night."

"I did." Liza strained to keep her voice down, to not wake Brody who was sleeping across the hall. "How about I fix some coffee? Come down when you're finished."

While the coffee brewed, she poured two glasses of orange juice and placed a box of muffins on the kitchen table. As quietly as possible, she put away last night's dishes from the dishwasher and wiped down the counters. She then went into the laundry room and began folding towels from the dryer.

Kate's slippers slapped against the ceramic tile as she came into the laundry room. "How much do you charge for your services?" J.B. was perched on her shoulder, enjoying a vigorous back rub.

"It'll be an even trade. Your advice for a bit of housekeeping." She folded a striped dishtowel and set it on the pile.

"Sounds fair."

After placing the baby in his swing, Kate flipped a switch and J.B rocked contentedly to "Three Blind Mice." Liza and Kate sat down at the kitchen table with their coffee and muffins. Kate took a long drink, sighed, and settled back in her chair.

"Okay, go. What's got you up so early?"

"I couldn't sleep."

"I figured that." Kate put her mug down, broke her muffin in half and wiped her hands on a paper napkin. "But, I'll need more information."

"Okay, so last night at the Brass Rail, Diana and her bitchy friends showed up. I never could stand those girls she ran around with in high school." Liza butchered her muffin into a pile of crumbs. "I could feel them watching me the whole night, whispering, all catty-like and—"

"Is there a point to this story? Because I planned to go back to bed once J.B. fell asleep."

"Sorry." She put two muffin chunks in her mouth and looked through the window, chewing slowly, mechanically. Kate tapped her arm as if there was a watch attached. Liza smiled at her, cheeks bulging. "Okay. Here it is." She washed the muffin down with coffee and pushed it away.

"Last night, Tucker overheard those bitches talking about him. They figured out he was my *boyfriend*." She air quoted with doubled fingers and then continued. "So, as soon as Diana came in, he came behind the bar and suggested we kiss—or did I?"

Kate's coffee cup thumped onto the table as she coughed into her napkin. "And did you?" she croaked.

"Yes. Because, you know, we're the Clauses and I'm supposed to be dating him, remember?"

Kate nodded and rolled her hand in the air. "Go on."

"So, I kissed him."

Kate waited a few beats. "And?"

"And he kissed me back."

"*And?*" Kate rested her elbows on the table and leaned toward Liza with her brows arched.

"And, I..." Liza slapped her hands on the table and slouched in her chair. "I liked it. Okay? Satisfied?"

"Yes, but were you? Satisfied?"

"Very funny. Look, okay, so I—" She popped out of her chair and marched around the kitchen island, staring down at her entwined fingers. "I wasn't expecting the kiss to be like that, you know. And I wasn't expecting to feel what I felt. I liked it. I more than liked it. It felt like..."

She stopped her trek and noticed Kate had lost interest in her muffin. She had her arms folded on the table and a tender smile on her face.

"It felt like we'd been kissing like that forever—like we *should've* been kissing like that forever. I can't explain it." She plopped back in the chair and shoved another chunk in her mouth.

"It didn't feel like two friends pretending to date. It felt right, like much more than friends," Kate said.

She bobbed her head up and down.

Narrowing her eyes, Kate considered Liza with a knowing grin. "Are you trying to tell me you think you're in love with Tucker?"

Her mouth still stuffed, she shook her head and mumbled, "Oh, God, no. Not love." She swallowed her muffin with a sip of coffee. "Absolutely not. I cannot fall in love with Tucker."

"Why? Tucker's a great guy and you two have been so close the past couple of years."

"Tucker is my friend. We're *friends*." Liza threw her head back, sucked in a deep breath, and planting her elbows on the table. "What if we started dating? And what if we broke up? Not only would I have lost a boyfriend, but I'd lose my friend, as well. I don't want to mess it up. Besides, I'm sure he feels the same way."

"You two need to talk about that kiss." Kate wrapped her hand around Liza's wrist. "Maybe he's just as physically attracted to you, too. Ask him."

"I can't ask him. I'm sure I'm just feeling this way because it's been so long."

"You wouldn't feel like that with just any guy."

"I shouldn't feel this way about Tucker. He's like a brother to me." She pulled her arm out of Kate's grasp and returned to circling the island, rubbing her hand up and down her thigh. "We've got to stop pretending. Something bad might happen. I'm cursed. This is a bad time of year."

"What are you ranting about?"

Liza threw her arms in the air. "Christmas, remember?"

Kate shook her head.

"The snow storm, the car wreck, the tree falling, the—I've told you about my bad luck. It's not a good time."

"I don't understand what you mean." Kate padded over to the coffee pot to refill her coffee. "One has nothing to do with the other."

"Think about it. Anything bad that has ever happened to me has happened at Christmas. Don't you think it's strange that now—right before Christmas—I'm having feelings for Tucker? Maybe this pretending stuff and keeping Diana and Bret from being Mr. and Mrs. Claus is setting me up for another disaster. If we give into our feelings—if he does feel the same for me—I just know something bad will happen. The fallen pine tree is just the beginning." Nervous energy surged through her fingertips. She waved her hands as if they could ward off evil spirits. "Maybe I didn't really feel anything when we kissed. It was just my imagination."

"You know what I think?" Kate set her coffee cup on the island and placed her hands on Liza's shoulders. She tensed as Kate hovered above her. "I think you're trying to come up with any excuse to not follow your heart. You're afraid to get hurt, afraid of a disaster. I get that. But this is Tucker we're talking about. If he feels the same for you, then I know he'll never hurt you or let anything bad happen."

"No, no." Liza's head shook as if she were having tremors. "Friends, that's all we are. Nothing more. We'll keep pretending until after the Mistletoe Ball and then tell everyone we've had an amicable break-up. By January we'll go back to the way things were."

"Do you think that's possible?"

"It has to be."

"Maybe you should break up sooner because if you all keep up this charade, you just might fall in love."

NINE

Someone bumped into Liza, causing her to stumble, knocking her fur stole off one shoulder. She readjusted her gray wig and wire-rimmed glasses, and mumbled under her breath, "How did I get myself into this?" She patted her wig back into place and rubbed her thick belly to be sure the pillow underneath her red velvet dress hadn't gone askew.

"Hello, Mrs. Claus." A little girl in a pink puffy coat waved to her as Liza pushed through the crowd toward the North Pole. She flashed a grandmotherly smile, but didn't stop to talk to the child. How had she let Tucker talk her into playing Mrs. Claus? Up ahead she spotted the life-sized gingerbread house where children could sit on Santa Claus's lap and collect candy canes from his wife at the annual Holiday Street Festival. Hopefully, the kids wouldn't notice this was her least favorite time of year. As she reached her post, Tucker glared at her through his wire spectacles and his white beard, and puffed out a sigh.

"I started to think you stood me up."

"Nope."

"The kids asked about you."

She shrugged, took her place on the ornate chair beside him, and picked up the box of candy canes, grateful the costume included thick, warm mittens. She had considered not coming, not so much because of Christmas, but because she was nervous about seeing him. Their kiss had been on her mind all day and she wasn't sure how to act around him.

Undeterred by the cold night air, a long line of children wrapped around the gingerbread house giving her little time to think about it.

As each child went through the line, telling Santa everything on their Christmas wish list, Liza handed them a candy cane and said "Merry Christmas." After several children had passed, she lifted the lace cuff on her sleeve to check the time, shocked to find she'd only be there twenty minutes.

"You have somewhere to be?" Tucker murmured out the corner of his beard-covered mouth.

"No."

"The night's just getting started."

"Mm."

"You mad at me or something?"

"No."

"You're talking in one-word sentences."

"Sorry." She scratched her head through the thick, curly wig that made her scalp tingle. Her muffin cap dropped to her shoulder.

"There you go again. I know you hate Christmas, but remember who got us into this in the first place."

"Believe me," she said as she stretched the cap over her wig. "I've been kicking myself ever since Thanksgiving."

"You can stop. I love playing Santa Claus." He lifted a toddler onto his lap and said, "What would you like for Christmas, little boy?"

As the young boy recited every toy he could think of, Tucker's eyes lit up as if fascinated with everything on the child's list. He was so good with the children and would make such a wonderful father someday. The corners of his eyes crinkled in a smile as he put the little boy back on his feet.

"Now, go get a candy cane from my *sweet* wife, Mrs. Claus."

Liza handed the boy a candy cane and glared at Tucker.

"It might help if you'd stop acting like such a Scrooge," he muttered.

"I'm being nice enough." The stupid wig felt like ants crawling around her scalp. "I can't take much more of this wig." She scratched so furiously, her cap popped off into Tucker's lap and her wire glasses dangled from her ears.

He snorted a laugh and turned his attention to three college girls giggling and nudging each other to sit on Santa's lap. "One at a time, ladies. Santa's only got one lap." he chuckled, thoroughly enjoying the pretty girls' attention. Liza folded her arms and angled her body away from the flirt-fest beside her as a sharp bout of heartburn flared in her chest. Why would it hit now? She hadn't eaten anything spicy.

"You sure you're not angry at me, Mrs. Claus?" he asked once the college girls received their candy canes. He waved his white glove at them as they walked away, casting suggestive glances at him as they strolled down the street.

"What? Because of those girls?" The puff of air she released ruffled the gray curls lying on her forehead.

"Who?"

"The ones who were drooling over you."

"Oh, so you're jealous?"

"Hardly." A stab of pain burned in her chest causing her to fold in half.

"You okay?" He rubbed his gloved hand over her back, and even through the thick fabric she reacted to his touch with a pleasant tingling in her belly. So much for believing it was all her imagination.

"I'm fine." She sat up and adjusted her wire-rimmed glasses, giving him a phony smile.

He furrowed his bushy white brows and then turned to lift a little girl onto his lap. "Hop right up here, young lady." He stroked his long beard and asked, "What would you like Santa to bring you this Christmas?"

"I'd like a bike and a cell phone and a…"

He leaned toward Liza and murmured out the corner of his mouth. "You act mad. Is it because of Christmas?"

"I told you it wasn't."

"Is it because of what happened at the bar last night?"

"Santa, are you listening?" The little girl tapped his shoulder, demanding attention.

"Ho, ho, ho. Of course, Santa's listening." He concentrated on the little girl's long list, nodding his head with each additional item.

"Of course not…" Liza snarled into his other ear. "Why would that bother me? That's a ridiculous thing to say."

"Seems like the only explanation to me," he whispered back, keeping his eyes locked on the little girl. She finally finished her long list of demands and he put her firmly on the ground in front of Liza.

"You should be nicer to Santa, you know," the little girl said as she held out her hand to receive a treat.

"Oh?" The box of candy fell to Liza's lap.

"Yeah. If you're not nice to Santa he won't give you what you want."

Tucker's raucous laugh could be heard a block away as he pointed at the little girl with an exaggerated wink. "You are a very smart little girl." He slapped a gloved hand on his knee and nudged Liza in the ribs. "Give her another candy cane, Mrs. Claus."

Satisfied her point was made and her extra treat received, the little girl ran across the street to her waiting parents. Tucker wiped the tears from his eyes, still laughing.

"It wasn't that funny." Liza snapped the lid on the plastic box and crossed her leg, angling away from him as he struggled to get his laughter in check.

"Think about it, Mrs. Claus." He draped a flowing velvet sleeve across her shoulders and pressed his mouth against her ear. "If you just admit that kiss was damned good, I'll give you what you want for Christmas."

The brush of his warm breath sent a quiver down her spine that had nothing to do with the fuzzy beard tickling her ear. His nearness was making it hard to stay grounded. It wasn't right, but what she wanted more than anything right now was another kiss. What was the matter with her?

"You couldn't give me what I want anyway." She shrugged his arm off her shoulder and turned her back to him.

"Try me. What do you want?"

No way would she confess she indeed wanted another kiss, nor could she tell him the second thing on her list—the castle. That, too, had to remain a secret, especially now that she knew she'd be competing against Bridges Enterprises. She couldn't tolerate doubts or allow anyone to talk her out of it.

"What I want you could never deliver."

"Don't think it will fit in my sleigh?"

She turned back around and caught his eyes twinkling, making him hard to resist. Maybe one more kiss, just to be sure she hadn't imagined it last night.

"It doesn't require a sleigh."

"A special type of delivery then?"

"Something like that."

She felt herself falling toward him as if pulled in by an invisible, magical force. She couldn't kiss him again. What if she liked it? What if she wanted more? It would ruin—

"Aren't you two darling? You make the cutest Mr. and Mrs. Claus." Virginia McNamara appeared out of nowhere, causing the box of candy canes to teeter on Liza's lap.

"Ho, ho, ho. Climb on Santa's lap, young lady." Virginia perched her hip on Tucker's knee and gave him a big hug. "What can Santa bring you this year?"

"Peace on earth?"

"I'd have to check with the elves on that one."

"Good will toward men and women?"

"Again, have to check with the head elf."

"How about simply you and Liza have a Merry Christmas? That's enough."

Tucker shifted Virginia more securely on his knee and locked his white gloves around her waist. "I'm more than willing, but I'm not so sure about *Mrs. Claus*." He cupped his hand around his mouth and pointed with his thumb toward Liza. "Not a fan of Christmas."

"Uh oh, is there a problem at the North Pole?" Virginia giggled and patted Tucker's stocking cap. "How about I put up the 'taking a break to feed the reindeer' sign so you two can get a snack or a drink."

"That's not necessary—" Liza began to protest.

"Great idea. Thanks, Virginia."

Virginia hopped off his lap like a woman half her age and retrieved the sign out of the gingerbread house. "There. The sign says you'll be back in fifteen minutes. Now go."

She went behind them, giving each a hearty shove in the back. "Go on."

He stood and held out his hand to Liza. "Come on. I'll buy you a beer, Mrs. Claus."

A white cloud puffed out of her mouth as she folded her arms across her chest, bypassing his hand, and plowed ahead of him. He followed her down the block to the Misty Mountain beer truck, which had a line snaked into the street. Brody and Travis were manning the taps, too busy to notice them.

"The line's too long," Tucker said as he grabbed her shoulders and steered her behind the truck.

He dropped his hold on her and pulled his white beard below his chin. "Okay, you go first."

"Go first? What do you mean? Why me?"

"Because you're the one who's pouting."

"I'm not pouting." She spread her hands across the puckered skirt of her red velvet dress, smoothing out imaginary wrinkles, feeling her lips do exactly that—pout. "Well, I guess…" She shook her head and cleared her throat as she tugged on her fur wrap. "I've been thinking…about last night."

"I thought that might be it." He tucked his gloves into the large pocket on the front of his costume and glanced across her shoulder. "I guess we should talk about the kiss."

"I guess we should." Her whole body began to shake from nerves. It was ridiculous. They had been friends for so long and never had a problem talking. Why did she suddenly feel so nervous?

"It was…I was a little surprised." He wouldn't look at her. Instead, he scanned the crowd passing through the middle of town. She didn't know what to say, so she stayed silent while he worked out his thoughts. "I didn't expect you to do what you did."

"Me?"

"I wasn't expecting you to kiss me like that."

"Well, you started it by coming behind the bar and kissing my hand in front of an audience. I just tried to be convincing."

"So, you were just laying it on thick for the crowd? Faking it?" Finally, he tore his gaze away from the crowd and looked directly at her.

"Yes...of course. Weren't you?" She squeezed and twisted the lacy cuffs in her hands, creating a tightly wound ball, leaving permanent wrinkles pressed into the fabric.

"I did my part," he said.

"I think we convinced Diana. Don't you?"

"No doubt."

"So, I'm not sure what else to say." It was all an act—just as it should've been. He didn't feel anything more for her than friendship. They were only friends and always would be. That was good. That was what she wanted. So why did she feel so disappointed?

"Did you like it?" He slipped his fingers in the band of her apron, drawing her closer while he kept his hooded gaze on her lips. A lightning bolt surged through her nether regions.

The moment of truth. The answer she'd been trying to deny. Yes, she liked it, more than she should have. This was Tucker—her brother's friend—almost like another brother to her. She shouldn't feel anything for him beyond admiration, kinship, or fondness. Yet, as they stood so close, discussing a kiss that she couldn't shake, all she could think about was doing it again.

"I, um, think...it was a great kiss," she said.

"Yeah?"

"Considering it was for show. How did you feel about it?"

"There's no doubt about it—you're a damn good kisser."

"It's weird to say this, but you're a good kisser, too."

"So…" His fingers slid back and forth under her apron band, creating a warm, inviting friction against her dress.

"So, we keep faking it, right? Whatever it takes to keep me out of hot water."

His warm breath brushed her cheeks like a seductive caress as he leaned in close.

"If you say so." Tucker brought his face closer to hers, and her body arched forward like a magnet to steel. Just a breath apart, she wrapped her arms around his neck and smothered his lips, wanting more of his incredible mouth. Just as he wrapped her tight in his arms, the spell was broken.

"Look, Mommy, Santa is kissing Mrs. Claus." A tiny voice drew them back to reality. Even though they were behind a truck, they were still exposed to the crowd. Liza broke out of his arms and buried her face in his chest. Velvet tickled her nose as she muffled a laugh into his costume. He quickly pulled his beard back onto his face and straightened his coat.

"Ho, ho, ho. You caught us, little girl." Most of Tucker's face was covered by the beard, but his cheeks burned red below his eyes.

"But there's not even any mistletoe." The little girl looked up at Santa, bewildered by their actions.

"There was, but I think Rudolph flew off with it." He grabbed Liza's hand and led her from behind the truck, patting the little girl on the head as they passed. "We're going to go find it. Come on, Mrs. Claus."

TEN

Liza took a sip of Misty Mountain's holiday brew, Grinch Grog, and stole a glance through the glass wall behind the bar, hoping to find Tucker checking on the fermenting tanks. She'd arrived at the brewery's holiday open house fifteen minutes ago expecting to find him greeting guests as they came in, but he had yet to make an appearance. Brody was acting as sole host, making sure everyone had a drink while answering their questions.

"Hey, don't you look gorgeous." Kate came up beside her, laying her hand on her shoulder. J.B.'s cheek was pressed to Kate's chest, fast asleep in his baby sling. "I love this dress." She ran her hand down a lacy sleeve, admiring the black dress Liza had paid a fortune for.

"Thanks."

"I'll be glad when I can wear nice things again. There's no point risking it with a drooling baby."

"It won't be long." J.B.'s cheek felt like warm satin as she glided her finger from his temple to his chin. "I like that you bring him everywhere. You don't let a baby hold you back."

"Right now he's very portable, so I'm not going to miss out on the holiday fun. Speaking of which, you're not dressed in your Mrs. Claus costume."

"Since this isn't a Chamber of Commerce event, we don't have to play Santa and the missus. I'm here as Tucker's date." Liza flicked her fingers in air quotes and rolled her eyes. "Gotta keep up the ruse. Usually I pour beer behind the bar, so there are perks to being in a *relationship*."

It felt strange saying they were in a relationship, but with every kiss she felt them heading toward something more than friendship—and it scared her to death.

"Have you seen him? I was supposed to meet him here." Liza glanced over Kate's shoulder as the door opened followed by a blast of cold air.

"No, I haven't. Maybe Brody's seen him."

"I'll ask him. See you later."

Liza walked toward the rough-hewn bar that lined the length of the tasting room. Brewing tanks stood behind the clear glass wall like enormous copper towers in a mini beer city. Two years ago, there were only two large vats, and now there were at least a dozen. Tucker had taken a hobby and turned it into a successful company. She hoped to have the same success with her gallery.

The bank had approved her loan and she was officially mortgaged to the hilt. If she didn't win the bid and make the gallery flourish, she'd have to take on a third job to pay her bills. She couldn't live with herself if she lost the little house Granny had left to her. Rather than be haunted by her grandmother, she'd like to have her smiling down because of her accomplishments. This had to work or Liza might find herself homeless and sleeping on a friend's couch.

Brody looked up from the tap where he was filling a pint glass with frothy ale. "You look nice."

"Thanks. Have you seen Tucker?"

"Probably still out back." He scraped the excess foam with a flat paddle and handed it to Travis who was seated at the bar.

"Out back?"

"In the RV," Travis said as he tipped the golden brew to his lips.

"What do you mean? What RV?"

"His home. His abode." Confusion must have been written all over her face because Travis continued his synonyms. "His dwelling. His domicile."

"For God's sake, Travis, what are you talking about?"

"Tucker's living in an RV behind the brewery." Brody finally answered her question, but it wasn't what she was expecting.

"Why is he living in an RV? His house is less than a mile from here."

"Not anymore." Travis tipped his forehead towards her, brows raised. "Now it's less than thirty feet from here." She didn't appreciate his annoying chuckle or being in the dark. None of this was making sense. Tucker never said anything about living in a camper behind the brewery. Brody was too busy pouring beer and Travis was enjoying himself too much to get any real answers. She'd have to get them herself.

She charged past the bar and into the back room, her four-inch heels tapping out a steady rhythm as she approached the back door. Surely this was a joke. There was no logical reason Tucker would live behind the brewery in an RV of all places. She pulled open the back door and stumbled onto the gravel behind the brewery. Sure enough, a small camper, circa 1970, was sitting beside the dumpsters and a tiny light glowed through the window.

Heels and gravel were not a good combination, but she did her best to teeter over to the RV without twisting an ankle. She pounded her fist against the aluminum door and was shocked to find Tucker on the other side, dressed in a sleek charcoal suit and burgundy tie. His dark hair was styled off his forehead and his face cleanly shaven. He was so mouthwateringly handsome she almost forgot he was standing inside a trailer with his head just inches from the ceiling.

"Tucker!"

"I was just on my way over." He stepped onto the top metal tread as she plastered her hands against his chest, giving him a firm shove backward.

"What is going on?" She stomped up the three metal stairs and slammed the door closed behind her. "Why are you out here? Why is there a camper behind your building?"

Turning slowly in a circle, she took in the tiny space, barely big enough for one person. His clothes were piled on an upholstered bench and his toiletries were laid out on a fold-down table. The bed, if it could be called that, had a narrow, thin mattress covered in rumpled sheets. When she let out a frustrated sigh, a puffy white cloud came from her mouth.

"It's freezing in here."

"Let's get to the party where it's warmer." She shrugged off the hand he'd wrapped around her wrist and folded her arms.

"We're not going anywhere until you tell me why you're living like a beatnik in a rundown RV with no heat in the middle of December behind the brewery when you have a perfectly lovely house less than one mile down that road and it only takes you three minutes to get to work so there is no way I'll believe you moved here to save time on your commute."

"Would you believe I wanted to downsize?"

"Tucker!" She stomped her foot knowing she must look like a petulant child, but she didn't like his cheeky attitude. Obviously, Brody and Travis knew he was living back here. Tucker told her everything. Why hadn't he told her he moved to this crappy, rundown trailer?

"I sold my house."

"Why?"

"I needed some cash."

"I thought the brewery was doing great. Why would you need cash? Does Brody know this? Of course, he does." She picked up a pair of socks from the only chair in the place, tossed them on the bed, and sat down. Her legs could no longer hold her. "Does he know why you moved back here? Did you ask him to lend you some money? I just don't unders—"

"Listen." He squatted in front of her, resting his hands on her knocking knees. "The brewery is fine. Brody is my partner and knows everything about our balance sheet. I'm planning a, um, an expansion and needed some cash, you know, so, um, to keep down lending costs. You understand?"

"A few too many ums and lack of eye contact. What's really going on?"

"I told you. I plan to expand and need the down payment."

"When did you decide this? Why didn't you tell me?"

"It's no big deal. Besides, Abby has been looking for a house, so I sold it to her. It was getting crowded at Mom's with her and the girls living there, and now they'll have a place of their own when Zack gets back from Afghanistan."

It made sense that his sister and husband would want their own home once he returned, but did it have to be Tucker's house? Couldn't Brody have pitched in some cash to help with the expansion? And why were they expanding again? They just doubled production last year.

Her jaw shook and her teeth chattered from the cold.

"You can't live here. There's no heat."

"As soon as Travis gets time to put in a thirty-amp service, I'll be able to plug in the camper and it will get toasty in here fast." She tried to ignore the nice feeling of his hands on her knees, rubbing warmth back into her legs through the thin fabric of her dress.

"In the meantime, you'll freeze to death. It's supposed to get in the teens over the next couple of days."

"I'll be okay. I've got my sleeping bag, the one I use when we hunt, and I spend most of my time in the brewery where it's warm. But I like the fact that you're worried about me."

He tipped his forehead toward hers and gave her thawing legs a playful squeeze. His lids lowered and he leaned closer, his mouth so tempting only an inch from her own.

"Does this thing even have a bathroom?" She brushed his hands from her legs and stood, nearly knocking him to the floor. She had to put some space between them. She was tempted to kiss him and they had to stop kissing. If they went much farther, their friendship would be ruined and she couldn't have that.

"Don't need one. I go in the brewery." He stood and straightened his tie, a bashful grin on his face.

"What about a kitchen?" He was so hot in that stylish suit she turned her back to get her yearning under control.

"I use the microwave in the break room."

"Honestly, you can't stay here."

"Where would you suggest I go? I'm too old to live with my mommy." He chuckled as he laid his hands on her shoulders.

"Could you move in with Travis?"

"He just has that small apartment over the garage. Might be cramped with the two of us."

"There has to be someplace other than this ice box."

He drew her back against his chest and his warm breath tickled her neck as he spoke softly against her ear. "I'll be fine."

"No, you won't."

"What would you suggest then?"

"Come live with me." It was out of her mouth before she realized what she had said.

"That's not such a good idea." His arms swallowed her body against his chest, creating a cocoon of warmth around her. "You're shivering. Let me warm you."

"Why won't it work?" The more he wrapped himself around her, the better the idea sounded.

"Let me hold you a minute and you'll warm up."

"I've got plenty of room. You could sleep in the downstairs bedroom." He was like a big, cozy furnace, his strong arms and solid chest giving off a blast of male heat she wanted to curl into. It would be nice to have him around on a cold night.

"Don't you think it would be awkward?" His warm breath tickled the back of her neck.

"Why? You've seen me in my PJs."

"When you were twelve." They shared a laugh and his breath against her skin was like a soft feather. "But I wouldn't mind seeing you in them again."

Maybe for just a minute she could rest her head back against his chest, just until she warmed up. There was no harm in that. Once she quit shivering, they would go to the party and act like the Christmas couple they were expected to be—without kissing. Kissing was where she drew the line, so it was best if she kept her back to him.

"So, Tucker, is that a yes?"

"Well, not necessarily."

The only part of her body still cold was her feet, but the rest of her body was warm and snug tucked up against him. It was so nice having his arms swaddled around her; she felt a little woozy. She could get used to this.

"Tucker, it'll be fine."

"I'm not sure."

She dragged her hair over one shoulder and tilted her head slightly, just in case he wanted to start a trail of kisses down her neck. What would be the harm in that? Just a few kisses below her ear. That would be nice.

"I wouldn't want it to get awkward between us," he said, resting his chin on the crown of her head.

"It won't."

He loosened his hold and took a step back. "Travis said he could put in the new outlet next week. I'll be okay."

Feeling abandoned, she drew his arms more tightly around her, drowning in the warmth of his body. "I'm still cold."

Again, she tilted her head to her shoulder, inviting his lips to skim her neck. All he had to do was lower his head just an inch or so and brush his luscious mouth below her ear. She felt drugged at the thought of it. "If you did live with me, we wouldn't have any problem keeping it platonic. We're just friends, remember?"

"Just friends. Right."

"We have to remain friends. That's most important." She covered his hands with hers, drew him in closer, and tucked them just below her breasts. This was okay, wasn't it? There was nothing wrong with snuggling up tight, keeping each other warm in this igloo. He needed her body heat, too. Keeping one hand below her breast, he spread the other across her stomach, pulling her spine tight against his chest and her butt against his bulging zipper.

"Absolutely. Our friendship is most important."

"See, I knew you'd agree. We've been friends so long. Nothing we do could mess that up." She wiggled her hips against his pelvis, feeling his desire against her backside.

"We won't mess up."

"So, there's no reason why you can't move in with me for a while." She pulled his hand from beneath her breast and pressed a kiss into his palm.

"Only if you're sure I won't be in the way."

"No," she sighed as his fingers did marvelous swirly things around her belly button. "You would never be in the way."

"Okay then, when should I move in?" He tugged her earlobe between his teeth and skimmed his lips down her neck. That's what she needed—just a little kiss or two to warm her up. Nothing wrong with that.

"Move in tonight. My house is nice and warm."

"Yeah?" His hand drifted north until it rested over her breast as his lips continued to flit down her neck. "You sure it'll be okay?"

"Absolutely."

His lips and hands were making her crazy. She flipped around and wrapped her arms around his neck, pulling him down for a deep, wet kiss. They shouldn't be doing this but, wow, was it nice. Right now, all she wanted was his mouth on hers and his hands right where they were, cupping her butt and drawing her in close. Her hands glided over the bunched muscles of his back, every ridge and contour solid under her palms.

How could she want him this much? Now was not the time to analyze her feelings. A moan escaped his throat and she drew him in deeper, the frosty chill now a fiery furnace.

All at once, the spell was broken by the rattling of the tin can camper. Someone was pounding on the door, causing the trailer to rock on his foundation.

"You all alright in there?" It was Travis outside the RV. She jumped out of Tucker's arms, embarrassed that they may have been seen through the camper's only window. He reached for the doorknob, but she drew him back and swiped her fingers over his lips, trying to remove her red lipstick from his mouth.

"Good enough. You can open it now."

"Are you trying to tear down the door?" Tucker barked as a blast of arctic air filled the camper.

"We were getting a bit concerned about you. Thought you might have hypothermia or something." Travis chuckled as he popped his head through the door and looked around. "But I can see the two of you are letting off enough heat to warm the place."

"Get out." Tucker laid his palm on Travis's natty head and pushed it out the door. "We'll be there in a few minutes." He slammed the door and turned back around, his cheeks red from the cold. "Where were we?"

"Stop." She halted his descent toward her mouth with a flattened palm to his rock-hard chest. The chill had cleared her brain...and her libido. She wasn't completely cooled off, but enough to think clearly. "We have to set some ground rules before you move in."

"Okay."

"What just happened, we can't let that happen again. Our friendship is too important. We need boundaries."

Even as she said the words, she didn't believe them. Maybe her head believed it, but the tingling below didn't. As long as they kept their hands to themselves, they should be able to live as roommates and maintain the friendship they'd always had. The last thing she wanted was to give him the wrong idea. She just hoped her body got on board with her brain.

ELEVEN

"Lucy, I'm home."

Liza dropped the paintbrush when she heard Tucker's silly Ricky Ricardo impression, creating a blue paint streak across the floor. She grabbed the brush and dropped it in a plastic bucket of water as the sound of thumping and banging echoed up the staircase. She rushed down the steps to find a large, prickly pine tree standing in the foyer. With a loud grunt, he emerged from behind the tree, a boyish smile plastered on his face.

"I got the tree."

"What do you mean? You know I don't decorate for Christmas."

"You are this year. Besides, that white pine out back needed topped out."

"But I don't have room."

"I made room."

"Tucker, I don't want a Christmas tree or any decorations. It's bad luck."

He heaved the massive tree across the room to a corner where an armchair once sat. "Can you hold the stand?" He pointed to a green tree stand and bent his knees, lifting the tree off the floor. "I need a little help here."

She blew out a sigh and marched across the room. "I don't do Christmas." She knelt on the floor and held the stand as he lowered the tree into the opening. He joined her on the floor to tighten the bolts into the trunk.

"I do. I'm going to help you fall in love with Christmas all over again."

"I doubt—"

"You used to like Christmas. I know. I found a box of ornaments in your attic."

"They belonged to my grandparents."

Still squatting beside her, he looked intently at her with his brows arched. "It's time to stop being a Scrooge and get back to celebrating the holiday you once loved."

"It's just so overdone, so commercial."

"It doesn't have to be." His face was an inch from hers. "We can keep it simple." His dark gaze drilled deep into her soul, causing a warm quiver from her stomach on south.

Keep it simple. That was good advice from a man who was making her life anything but simple. Tucker had moved in three days ago, taking the downstairs bedroom where her grandparents once slept, and hadn't touched her or made a single advance, much to her frustration. How did he stay so cool, such a complete gentleman? All she could think about was leaping into his arms. They agreed that their friendship was paramount and nothing would get in the way of it, no matter how tempting—and she had been tempted, more than once—like right now. Just another couple inches and she could taste his mouthwatering kiss. Was he thinking the same thing?

"We can do that." She felt herself falling toward him, hoping he'd make the first move. "Keep it simple." She hoped he was talking about the two of them and not Christmas decorations.

"I'm willing if you are." He narrowed the divide, lowering his lids as he grew closer. Her body zinged with anticipation, ready for his soft lips to meet with hers. She had promised it wouldn't be awkward between them and it hadn't been. They hadn't been this close to each other since the night in the camper. Maybe it wouldn't hurt to have one little kiss. Liza inched closer.

"Hey, bud, how do you want me to hang these lights?" Travis blurted, coming through the front door without knocking. He had the most uncanny sense of timing.

"Shit." Tucker's laughter broke the spell and she sat back on her heels, only partially relieved Travis had once again interrupted them.

"You're not hanging lights on my porch, are you?" She protested, but his crooked grin and flushed cheeks washed away her anger.

"Tucker thought it would brighten up the place."

"There's no point." Liza stood and parked her fists on her hips. "No one will see it but me."

"And Brody and Kate and the baby. If you want to be the fun aunt, you've got to decorate for Christmas."

"I'm J.B.'s only aunt and he's too young to notice."

"Do it for me then." Tucker pulled her hands from her hips and enveloped them in his. "I love Christmas lights. You won't deny me this simple pleasure, will you?" He was so damned adorable with his crooked grin and his melted-chocolate eyes, how could she say no?

"Fine." She tugged her hands from inside his and raked her fingers through her hair. "A Christmas tree and lights outside. That's it. No kitschy snowmen or tacky elves. No Kris Kringle knickknacks or any other decorations. Agreed?"

"Agreed." He extended his hand to seal the deal and even that gesture, with his palm pressed against hers, set fireworks exploding through her body. Even the most innocent of touches drove her mad. She wanted nothing more than to tug him into her arms and lay a long, tantalizing kiss on his lips. She was falling and had never been more scared in her life. Why couldn't she follow her own advice and kept it platonic, just friends? And why wouldn't her body cooperate?

Later that night, after the tree was decorated and the lights strung along the porch roof, Liza lay in her bed with the comforter pulled up under her chin. She settled against the pile of pillows with a book in hand. After the close encounter earlier today, she had decided it best to read alone in her room and avoid being near Tucker. She was finding it harder and harder to be alone with him, craving another heart-stopping kiss and struggling to keep her lust under control. There was something wrong with her. She shouldn't be having these feelings about him.

She opened her novel to page one and read the first sentence. A quiet tap on her door drew her away from the story, sending a nervous quiver down her spine. The tapping continued, followed by "Liza." He was knocking on her door, aware she was awake by the light streaming under the door. She set her book aside and pulled the covers tightly under her chin.

"Come in."

He opened the door and rested his shoulder against the wood frame. "Sorry to bother you." He was wearing a thin T-shirt and pajama pants. His bare feet were crossed at the ankle and his arms folded over his chest, making his biceps bulge. Her mouth went dry. Obviously, he knew his warm, sleepy presence was affecting her because he smiled and crossed the room where he perched a hip on her bed and picked up the book.

"What're you reading?"

Embarrassed, she grabbed the book out of his hand, hoping he didn't see the bare-chested Highlander on the cover.

"Never took you for the romance type."

"It's not exactly romance." She shoved the book in her nightstand and sat up straight in her bed, making sure her comforter was covering her breasts. "I like the historical setting."

His smile said he didn't quite believe her.

"There's a Stephen King movie on in ten minutes. Thought maybe you'd like to watch it with me."

Great. Just what she needed: to sit on the couch with Tucker, gripping his hand in fear, waiting for the suspense to build while she buried her face in his chest—his firm, solid, tempting chest.

"It's kind of late."

"Since when is nine o'clock late?"

"Don't you have to get up early tomorrow?" She gripped the cotton linens in her hands so tight her fingers went numb.

"I think I can stay up until eleven and still get plenty of sleep."

"Well, I, um—"

"Are you afraid?" He tapped gently on her nose and gave her a wry grin.

Not of Stephen King.

"Don't worry. I'll protect you from the scary demons."

That's not what I'm afraid of. Her eyes drifted around the room.

"Well." She flinched when he patted her thigh through the thick covers. "If you change your mind."

Before he made it to the door, she sat up, letting the comforter fall to her waist, but keeping her leg safely hidden.

"Are you making popcorn?"

"Of course. Have I ever let you down?" he cocked a crooked grin at her and padded down the stairs.

No, Tucker had never let her down, but if she didn't get her head on straight, she'd let him down. A moment ago, when his hand smothered her thigh, she inwardly cringed, knowing what he didn't about the mangled mess the wreck had left her in. Throwing off the covers, she stared at the red, angry, jagged scar that covered her left leg from hip to knee. A piece of metal had ripped through her flesh, laying her muscle wide open to the broken femur inside. The third surgery had resulted in an infection so severe the wound had to heal from the inside out, leaving a wrinkled, bumpy trough in the center of her thigh. It was so hideous it was still hard for her to look at it. Tucker could never see it. If he was going to continue to live here, she had to get her urges under control.

She pulled on pink pajama bottoms, a pale gray hoodie, and her fuzzy slippers, determined to simply watch the movie. She could handle this. She and her *friend* had watched plenty of movies together and nothing had happened. It was time to stop hiding in her room.

***

Sparks flared and flames roared as Tucker tossed another log on the fire. The Christmas tree and the fire gave off the only light in the room. He set the bowl of popcorn in the middle of the couch and settled himself on one end, doing his part to stay within the boundaries of friendship like they agreed. With any luck, she'd throw the popcorn bowl to the floor and climb onto his lap.

"So, which movie is it?" Liza rounded the sofa and plopped next to the bowl, tucking her heels behind her as she reached for a handful of popcorn.

"*The Shining.*"

"Here's Johnny," they blurted out simultaneously and fell into laughter. He'd missed the comfortable, relaxed feeling between them. Nervous around her the last couple of days, he awkwardly side-stepped her whenever she was within inches of him. He had promised to keep their friendship front and center, and wouldn't do anything to mess it up. But damn if it wasn't getting harder to resist her. The only thing holding him back was the fear of getting shot down again. If she wanted anything more than friendship, he'd wait for her to give the green light.

Once the movie started, they silently munched and kept their eyes locked on the screen. As the popcorn disappeared, he noticed Liza's fear building. He set the empty bowl on the coffee table and laid his hand on the sofa where the popcorn had set. Whenever they'd watched a scary movie before, she had gripped the life out of his hand, and he was hoping she'd need it again.

Slowly, as each terrifying scene intensified, he noticed her inching closer to him. He switched positions, draping his arm across the sofa back, bending in her direction, making it easier for her to fall into him.

"Oh, crap. I hate this part." She scooted to the center of the sofa and curled into a ball, tucking her face into her sweatshirt. Only her blue eyes peeked out.

"This is ridiculous." He moved closer and wrapped his arm around her. "Come here." She molded into his side, keeping her face pressed against his chest while keeping her eyes on the screen. "You never could get through this movie, you big chicken."

"Shh. He's about to ax down the door." When she snuggled tighter, he wrapped his other arm around her and drew her in close. He took a contented breath, inhaling the sweet floral scent of her silky, now-lavender hair, which brushed against his cheek. How perfect she felt in his arms, like she belonged there. How would she react if tonight he made the first move?

"Get ready." She squealed into her fists as she closed her eyes. "I hate this part."

"Why are you afraid of this? You've seen it a hundred times." His chuckle ruffled the top of her head.

"Tell me when it's over." She curled tighter, slipping her arms around him. Her nose and mouth were smashed against his ribs, her muffled screams vibrating against his skin. A vacuum cleaner commercial came on, temporarily halting the drama.

"Okay, break time. You can come up for air now." She slowly uncurled out of his arms, leaving a disappointing void where she'd just been. "Look at you. Your nose is all red." He tenderly traced the length of her nose to its perky little tip. He wanted to kiss her so badly, but he'd promised himself he'd hold back. "You okay?"

She replied with a small nod and moved back, allowing a foot of space between them. "Maybe we should turn this off. I know how it ends."

Tucker pressed the off button, leaving them in the soft glow of the tree and fire. Outside the wind whipped, making the old house creak and the storm windows rattle. He dropped the remote on the coffee table and settled back into the sofa. Liza was looking at him—her lips slightly parted as if a word silently hung there.

"Not as tough as you used to be," he said, patting her on her bent knee.

"I scare more easily, I guess." She pulled her knee from under his hand and sat up straight, keeping her eyes locked on the fire.

"What scares you? Besides that movie."

"Just…" She brought her thumb to her mouth and gnawed on its cuticle. "Stuff."

"What kind of stuff?"

"I don't know." She popped off the couch and paced in front of the coffee table. "Life. Things going wrong. You know." Her arms flew out and she turned to face him. "Stuff."

"Can you be more specific?" He walked around the coffee table and placed his hands on her shoulders. She spooked under his touch.

"No. I can't."

"Are you afraid of me?"

"Of course not. That's ridiculous." She attempted to turn away, but he held her firmly in his grasp. Though she had avoided any alone time with him for the past three days and treated him like a houseguest, it was obvious she was fighting her desire just as he was.

"Then why have you been avoiding me?"

"I haven't been avoiding you."

"Why are you so mad right now?"

"It's just..." She jerked back and walked into the kitchen. Tucker followed her and stood in the doorway as she rummaged through the refrigerator. "It's different between us. That's all."

She pulled out a bag of apples and dumped them into the sink. She held each apple under the water and rubbed so hard her whole body shook. No dirt or pesticides would survive her furious scrubbing.

"Ever since." She jerked open a drawer and rifled through its contents, creating a loud clanking of utensils. "Damn it. Where's the paring knife?"

He crossed the room and opened the dishwasher, handing her the knife from inside. He leaned against the counter and watched as a long, thin apple peel grew in her hand. She was moving so quickly, he was afraid she'd eventually cut herself, so he took the knife and apple away from her.

"Let me do that." He set the apple on a cutting board, splitting it into eight wedges. "Here." He handed a piece to her and she bit it in half.

"You were saying. Ever since...what?" He stuffed a piece in his mouth, watching her struggle to talk about their current situation. She had to be the one to spill her feelings and start the conversation. The last time he had tried, the night of her wreck, she'd made it very clear they would never be anything more than friends. But lately, even though she continued her friendship-only mantra, her body chanted something more. If she was indeed falling in love with him—and, God, he hoped so—she needed to be the one to confess it.

"It's just that…" She tossed the other half of her apple chunk in the sink and braced her hands on the counter, gazing at her reflection in the kitchen window. "Everything is different between us. Ever since…"

"Ever since we kissed that night at the bar?"

"Yes. And at the street fair. And in the camper." She slammed her palms on the counter and turned toward him, rubbing her hand over her thigh. "It shouldn't be like this. We're friends. We've been friends for so long. It's never been awkward between us and I don't like it."

"Would you like me to move out?"

"And live in that ice box? No." She grabbed his arms, giving them a hearty shake. "No. I've loved having you here. I don't even mind the Christmas tree. It's been great. So great…" Liza dropped her grip as her voice faded. "But strange."

"How so?"

"Damn it, Tucker. Why do you keep asking me these questions?"

"Because I think there's something you want to tell me, but you're afraid of my reaction." He stepped toward her, closing the gap between them, and brushed his knuckle against her cheek, hoping to make it easier on her. "You know you can tell me anything." He fingered a pale lavender strand behind her ear, letting his fingertip trail down her neck. "You can't scare me off."

"You want to bet?"

TWELVE

Liza shoved the well-washed apples back into their clear plastic bag and crossed the kitchen to the refrigerator. She deposited the bag in the fruit drawer and slammed the door shut. Tucker was hovering over her, demanding answers, his eyes pleading with her, and his gentle touch sending shock waves to the tips of her toes. Why couldn't he just let it go? He didn't need to know how she fanaticized about ripping his clothes off and running her hands down his taut, rippled six-pack. Or how she'd wake in the middle of the night in a cold sweat from a dream starring him and her locked in a torrid kiss, and his look of horror when she took off her clothes. She needed to get her urges under control.

She marched to the living room, picked up the iron poker, and feverishly stabbed into the glowing logs.

"Let me have that." He extracted the poker from her hand, nudging her away from the fireplace. He repositioned the logs, setting them to burn down and then returned the poker to its holder. "Now." He turned to her. "Talk. We know everything there is to know about each other."

"Not everything." She went to the Christmas tree and tapped a silver bell ornament. Its tiny ding the only sound in the otherwise silent room. "You have to stop pretending."

"Pretending?"

"Pretending to be my boyfriend."

"Why? Mr. and Mrs. Claus are supposed to be a couple."

"You just do."

"Why?" He sidled behind her and she melted to his warm breath in her hair.

"Would you stop asking why?"

"Explain it."

"It's too realistic, okay?"

"Too realistic?" With his hands on her shoulders, he turned her around to face him, tearing her away from the colorful bulbs and trinkets on the tree.

"Yes. You put too much into it."

He blew out a hearty chuckle and settled his gaze back on Liza. "You're the one who slipped her tongue in my mouth that first night." His hands slid languidly down her arms until he captured her hands in his. "I'm not complaining, by the way. But, if we're pretending, it shouldn't affect our friendship, right?"

"It's just that—"

"Yes?" He leaned down, bringing his face closer to hers.

"It's hard to—"

"Mm-hm?" He inched closer.

"I can't seem to—"

"Resist?" He brought his lips a breath away from hers. She felt a tug of war going on inside her head. She craved his kiss, but knew if they kept this up it would ruin everything and she couldn't lose his friendship. This had to stop. She flattened her hands on his chest and shoved, causing him to stumble into the sofa.

"That's what I'm talking about. You can't do that. We're pretending, remember?"

Tucker pushed himself to a standing position and then perched on the arm of the couch. "What if we stopped pretending?"

"Yes. We'll stop pretending and tell Diana and Bret and the committee we're just friends. We'll set a new precedent. Mr. and Mrs. Claus can just be friends. That will be better."

"That's not what I meant." She refused to look at him, to give in to the sultry tone of his voice. By the tingling through her body, she knew he was watching her, expecting her to question his definition of pretending.

"What about the fact that I live here?"

"What about it?" She gathered a stack of magazines in her arms, aligned their edges, and placed them back on the coffee table.

"Won't it seem strange when you tell them we're only friends but we're living together?"

"At least you won't be required to kiss me."

"I believe I am required to kiss you under the mistletoe at the ball."

"Again, we can start a new tradition."

"I don't mind. In fact, you seem to like kissing me."

"Stop it, Tucker." She stopped her fidgeting and glared at him. He had a sexy, irresistible grin on his face making her palm itch. She wanted to slap him—or run her fingers over his taut muscles—she wasn't sure which. "This isn't real. It's make-believe. It stops now." She gathered the coasters tossed across the end table, stacking them into perfection.

"I agree. The pretending stops now." He took the pile of coasters out of her hand, placing them silently on the end table. He gathered her quivering hands in his and tugged her in his direction. "I think what's making you so angry is that you like it when we kiss."

"That's not it."

He placed his arms around her waist and pulled her between his knees. "When you kiss me, you react in a way that makes me think you're enjoying it."

"Tucker...you need to stop."

"Why?" He pulled her closer and his fingers drew lazy circles on her back, sending white heat through her belly. "Don't you like kissing me?"

Of course, she liked it. Who wouldn't? A big, strong, sexy man had his arms around her and all she could think of was drowning in his kiss. How could any woman resist that? Carnal lust. That was all it was.

"In fact. I think what's scaring you is the fact..." He ran his fingertip across her collar bone. "You like it a lot."

She jumped back like she'd been burned with the hot fire poker. She slapped his arms away and crossed hers over her chest. Aggravating tears filled her eyes while fear surged through her. She shook her head as she stared at Tucker, whose eyes were lit with amusement. They were playing with fire and it wouldn't end well.

"It's okay." He reached for her, but she took another step back. "I like kissing you, too."

"Stop it, Tucker. We shouldn't do this. The only reason we like it is because we've both been alone too long."

One foot in front of the other, he followed her as she backed toward the kitchen. His head nodded and his eyes sparkled. "Maybe. Or maybe it's more than that."

"No."

"Are you sure?"

She frantically shook her head. She couldn't give in to his sexy, gravelly voice and bedroom eyes. Friends. That's all they were. That's all they could be. Any more and they would ruin everything.

"What's gotten into you, Tucker? Don't come any closer."

"I'm just saying if you want to kiss me, you know, to see if it's anything or not, you can." He continued his slow trek toward her, matching each of her backward steps. "You're right though. We've both been alone too long."

She couldn't go any farther. Her back hit the wall between the Christmas tree and the kitchen doorway, and Tucker was inches away. What if she confessed she was falling for him, but he only expected sex? Friends with benefits would never work for her, but, admittedly, she was finding it harder to resist him. Of course, once he saw the scarring and he knew the truth, he wouldn't want her.

"I'm cursed this time of year," she murmured as he inched closer.

"Why do you always say that?" He pulled her against him while tracing the outside of her face with the back of his hand.

"I've told you. Whenever things are going great for me this time of year, something bad happens. You know my history."

"Are you saying something good is happening between us?"

"Well, I mean, we've both admitted we're pretty good kissers."

"For sure." The growl in his voice and his gooey chocolate gaze made her knees go weak.

"Maybe it's the pretending or the season or the cold wind outside or—"

"What are you babbling about?"

"I just…" The cinnamon aroma from a burning candle and the soft glow of the Christmas lights playing off his dark, shiny hair, made her senses crackle like the pops and snaps of the burning logs. "I want to…"

"Kiss me?"

"Yes." It came out on a sigh and she sagged into the wall.

He closed the gap until just an inch stood between them, his eyes locked on hers. "You're my best friend and will continue to be, there's no harm in being together."

"But what if—"

He lifted her in his arms, letting her feet dangle between his legs.

"Listen to me." With one hand firmly around her back, he cupped her head with his other. "We're obviously attracted to each other, but I'll stop if you really want me to." He was nose-to-nose with her.

"It's just…"

"Tell me you don't feel it."

"So, I…"

"Tell me."

All the fight left her body. She had nothing left. She wrapped her arms around his neck and smothered her mouth against his shoulder. "I can't." She raised her head, could feel her face contorted with anguish. "But I—"

Tucker shook his head, stifling her protests. "But you feel something, right?"

She stared into his deep brown eyes and found herself nodding, as if her head and neck had a mind of their own.

"Good, so it's not my imagination." He kissed her quick. "You want me as much as I want you." He gave her another fast kiss. "Just say the word."

This time there was nothing quick about it. He lowered his head, brushing a soft, slow kiss on her lips, and if he didn't have her firmly encircled in his arms, she would have puddled to the floor. It was the first time he'd initiated intimacy between them, but even now he had more control than she did. Her hands circled his neck and she smashed her mouth against his. Whenever he came near, she wanted to blanket herself around him, press him against her, kiss him with all her strength. He followed her lead and kissed her deeper, more powerfully than ever before, and she tightened her hold on him. His tongue tangled with hers while he grabbed a handful of her hair, holding her head in place. Their tongues plunged, groped, intertwined, sucked away their breath as if their very existence counted on this kiss. His hand slid lower, palming her bottom, drawing her closer to him. She needed to touch him, feel his warmth.

She slid her hand inside his T-shirt, running her fingers up and down his back. He moaned happily and she wrapped her other hand around his neck. She couldn't get deep enough, couldn't get enough of him, and right now, all her other worries were gone. He tucked both hands under her butt, urging her legs around his waist, and carried her to the sofa. Their mouths stayed locked as he lowered her against the arm, propping her against the pillow. She stretched out her legs and he did the same, lying over her, keeping his weight off her by bracing himself on the back of the couch.

She tugged him down, relishing the full length of him crushing her into the sofa cushions. His hand trailed from her butt down the back of her thigh, creating a lava-hot burn through the thin fabric of her pajama pants. This was what she'd wanted, dreamed of since that first kiss at the bar. Though she demanded they remain friends, she was the one who had crossed the line.

He bent her knee and eased himself between her legs. She spread her fingers over the back of his head and pulled him deeper, her tongue demanding more. She wanted him so badly, but when he tugged down on the waistband of her pajama pants, a bright, white light flared behind her lids. Her breath caught and her chest clenched. She had to stop him before he saw.

"Tucker." She tried wiggling out of his grasp and into a sitting position, but this only seemed to encourage him. If he saw her deformed thigh, with its hideous scar, he would be repulsed and wouldn't want to touch her again. She was falling so hard, his shock and disgust would crush her.

"Yeah, babe."

"Don't." She wedged her hands between them and pushed him off. "No. I want you to stop."

THIRTEEN

Shot down again. All the blood in his body had rushed to one tender, extremely sensitive area; they'd been so close to consummating years of his fantasies. He should have known better than to get his hopes up.

Liza placed her hands on either side of his face, willing him to stop, forcing him to look at her. Her face blurred in his delirium. "I have to tell you something."

"You don't have to say anything." She'd told him no once before. Why the hell would he think she'd want him now? He wasn't sure why she kissed him the way she did if friendship was all she wanted.

"It's important."

He breathed heavily, struggling to catch his breath. "I know already. We're just friends. I get it."

"Whatever we are—"

"Just say it." He continued to draw in deep breaths as she turned her face to the fire breaking eye contact.

"We can't sleep together."

"I wasn't thinking of sleeping." He mumbled as he pushed himself away and sat up, covering his lap with a pillow. Nothing should *stand* in the way of whatever she was about to say.

"I'm not—I don't think you'll want to—you should know—"

Finally, the glassy, love-swamped blur cleared from his vision and he looked at her. She was still staring at the fire with a fist clenched between her teeth and her other hand rubbing circles into her thigh. "What's wrong?"

"I've never…I've never had sex."

"Huh?" He braced his hands against the arm of the couch, caging her prone body beneath him. "You're a virgin?"

"Yes." Her cheeks were as red as the fire's flames.

"How's that possible?"

"Well, I never—"

"I get that, but you've dated. How the hell did they keep their hands off you?"

She smiled at the compliment and finally looked at him. She lifted herself into a sitting position and pulled the pillow from behind her back, gripping it in her hands.

"I just always thought I would wait until marriage. Or at least until I met someone I wanted to do it with."

"That's admirable." Settling back into the cushions, he ran his hand through his hair and stretched out his legs, returning the pillow to his lap.

"You're mad."

"I'm not mad," he snapped, but then muttered, "Just turning blue."

"Oh, God, so it's true."

"What's true?"

"The rumors. What they said about me in high school. I didn't mean to be a tease."

"You're not a tease." *Try telling that to my little friend hiding under the pillow.* Seriously, one thing for sure about Liza, she was honest, outspoken and never played games. He didn't know why she kissed him the way she did, but she wasn't intentionally trying to torment him.

"That's what people always said about in me in high school. Maybe it's true. Maybe I'm frigid."

Tucker burst out laughing and gathered her worried face in his hands. "Is that what they said?"

"That was my word. No passion. What I remember them saying was I wouldn't put out."

While still laughing, he leaned in and pressed his lips to hers. "Baby, I'm glad you didn't *put out*. Trust me you've got way too much passion to call yourself frigid."

"That's it. I'm too aggressive, but never seem to follow through. Why are you still laughing?"

"Liza, would you stop?"

"You said it yourself. You're turning blue. Maybe Bret was right about me."

"Hey, don't believe anything that asshole said about you. He was the one who was too aggressive that night, who demanded more than he should. He had no right to treat you the way he did and then start awful rumors about you."

"But, why did he—"

"Because his ego was crushed by a beautiful, respectable girl. He couldn't let his buddies think you'd turned him down so he told them you were a tease." Tucker kissed her lips, her nose, each cheek, and her forehead.

"Wait, how did you know? We've never talked about that before."

"I know when those rumors started. I was there."

"The night of my wreck?"

"Yeah."

"I don't remember anything after turning Bret down."

"I skated down the river and found you crying on the bank."

"I was crying? Over Bret Bridges?"

"Yes."

"I can't believe that."

"He said some really terrible things to you."

"I told you that?"

"Yes, you told me everything that happened. How he was pressing you to have sex right there on the river bank and you told him no. While we were out on the ice, we could hear him and his buddies laughing around the fire. He was probably starting that crap about you. I'm not sure if he said anything else to you later, but it wasn't long after that you wrecked your car."

He must have said too much. Liza jumped off the sofa, grabbed the fire poker, and prodded the burning logs.

"Why haven't we ever talked about that night? You never told me you were there."

"I figured it was best we didn't."

Because you'd made it crystal clear I'd never be anything more to you than a friend.

"I'm so confused. Sometimes, just before I wake up in the morning, I have these flashes of memories, but nothing I can piece together. All I remember is him trying to force me into having sex, being mad, and that's it."

"Still don't remember getting into your car?"

"No, but I remember the headlights coming at me and Diana screaming. Why can't I remember anything else?"

He crossed the room, set the fire poker in its holder, and pulled Liza into his arms, smoothing hair away from her face. Her wide-eyed, blank gaze searched for answers, but he couldn't explain why certain events from that night were blocked from her memory. She curled into his embrace and he laid his cheek against her silky head. Brody had told him the doctors believed there was a chance her memories of that night would return. Would it help jog her memory if he told her the things she said to him that night? It might help her, but it would leave him broken all over again. If she remembered what she'd said to him that night, it just might reinforce her vow to remain only friends.

Tucker went into the office early the next morning to avoid Liza. Last night had been frustrating and confusing for both of them, but for very different reasons. Working through a pile of invoices, he hoped to get his mind off what almost happened last night and the déjà vu moment when she pushed him away.

Plugging numbers into the accounting software was a painstaking process, one that required his full attention. Bookkeeping was not one of his strengths—making beer was. The brewery was doing better than projected, so maybe it was time to bite the bullet and hire an in-house accountant. Brody would be on board with the decision. Besides, opening the new pub would eat up any extra free time—time he had hoped to spend with Liza. But, after last night, he was sure they would go back to being just buddies.

He crossed the office and rolled out the architect's drawings onto the conference table. His plans were to develop another commercial block at the end of Main Street with the castle front and center as a traditional English pub, flanked on either side by additional retail space. The architect had done a great job of incorporating the turn-of-the-century style of other in-town buildings with the gray granite fortress. If all went according to plan, his name would be called at the Mistletoe Ball as the winner of the bid.

His cell phone buzzed, pulling his focus from the blueprints and onto the screen where Travis's name was emblazoned.

"You're at it early this morning," Tucker said before taking a sip from his coffee mug.

"Yeah, got a lot on my plate today. You still want that thirty amp installed at the back of the brewery?"

"Sure, if you've got time." He had hoped to tell Travis things were going so well at Liza's he didn't need it. If only he could figure out what was going through that crazy blue or pink or lavender head of hers. She kissed him like her life depended on it, obviously aroused and ready, but then threw on the brakes. Why was she hanging on to this pledge to remain friends—and celibate?

"I'll try to get over there first thing tomorrow morning. Hey, while I have you on the phone, I heard in the Sit and Sip this morning three bids were submitted for the Leaks-a-Lot. Who the hell would want to take on that monstrosity?"

"Three? I heard Bridges Enterprises was bidding and they want to tear it down for a gas station."

"According to scuttlebutt down at the coffee shop, there are two bidders who want to renovate the castle and one wants to turn the rest of the block into a dog park."

"A what?"

"Yeah, not sure what they plan to use the building for but they want to put in benches and such, and let dogs run around loose."

"Hmm. I thought the bids were sealed. Who told you all this?"

"I overheard Arthur and Rodney talking. They're both on the committee."

"Overheard? Or were you eavesdropping?"

"Could I help it if they were talking a little loud?"

"Shit." Tucker slammed the tube of blueprints against the table. "Talk about a conflict of interest. Rodney's daughter is dating Bret Bridges. They'll probably give the construction contract to Rodney to build the station."

"What's it to you?"

"I just don't want to see the old place torn down, that's all."

"But can you imagine how much it would cost to renovate that place?"

He could imagine, all right. In fact, even with selling his house, he'd need to take out a loan to complete the project. His carefully designed business plan promised a profitable enterprise as long as everything fell into place. Maybe it was time to do a little politicking and talk to his allies, Arthur and Virginia, who were both on the committee. He had put too much time and money into this project to let it go to the dogs.

***

"So, wasn't I right?" Liza threw her arms out to her sides and spun in a circle in the middle of the dusty old castle, her voice echoing off the thick plaster walls. "Isn't this a great space? Just a little elbow grease and it'll be beautiful. What do you think of it, Darla?"

With her head tilted back, the local realtor the committee had entrusted to show the castle to potential bidders, turned slowly, taking in the height of the massive building.

"If you think it'll work as a, well, whatever you think it should be, who am I to argue?" Darla drifted toward the back of the hall, looking up at the ceiling where pigeons roosted on the window sills. "All I know is three people have plans for this place, but none have them told me. I just get paid to show it."

Liza had called Darla this morning and asked if she could show her the castle again. She needed to take one last look before she signed off on the final changes to the blueprints. So far she was on budget and didn't want to waste any of the money she'd borrowed on endless design revisions.

"I've submitted my plans to the committee and so have Bridges Enterprises, but who else?"

"I don't know who submitted bids, but I know who I've shown it to and I'm obligated to keep that information confidential."

"Well, I know Bridges Enterprises is hoping to build another one of their convenience store gas station monstrosities here because Bret told me. That would ruin the historical presence of downtown."

Darla smiled like she was trying to hide the fact that she had a pair of queens and a jack in her hand, but didn't say a word.

"Right? There is no way the committee would choose them over my plans to restore the building."

"Bridges isn't the only one you need to worry about."

"What do you mean?" Fear streaked down Liza's back. Darla knew more than she was letting on.

"You didn't hear this from me, but I've heard the third bidder plans to tear down the castle and build retail space along the whole block."

"They can't tear it down. My idea is the best one. Restore the castle and turn the first floor into an art gallery and use the top floor for art classes."

Whoops. She just spilled the beans. Darla's mouth hung open, and Liza braced herself for the negative comments that would shake her confidence.

"An art gallery? What a great idea."

"Really?" She nearly fainted with relief. "You like it? On the outside, I want to turn the rest of the block into green space and a sculpture garden where folks can gather on sunny afternoons, walk their dogs, and relax around a fountain."

"It sounds lovely." Darla tucked her leather portfolio under her arm, indicating the showing was over. "If anyone can pull it off, it's you. If you'd like me to talk to the committee on your behalf, I'll be glad to do that, if you think it would help."

"Thanks, Darla. I'd like that. I need all the help I can get to save the castle."

Liza felt like she was walking on air. She'd kept her idea to herself for fear someone would talk her out of it, but Darla's enthusiasm made her confidence meter go through the roof. She wondered what Tucker would think of her plans. He knew what it was like to have a dream and bring it to fruition. She was sure he had encountered a few doubters when he started the brewery, but look what a success he'd become. Maybe tonight she'd let him in on her little secret.

Fourteen

The smell of sugar and vanilla tickled Tucker's frost-bitten nose as he came inside, shaking frozen rain pellets off his coat. The drive to Liza's from the brewery had been treacherous as the roadways became covered with a thin sheet of ice. The blazing fire and the twinkling tree lights seemed to keep rhythm with the upbeat Christmas music blasting from the speakers. Had he walked into the wrong house?

He hung his coat in the hall closet and tiptoed toward the kitchen where he found Liza elbow-deep in sudsy water, humming along and swinging her hips to "Rockin' Around the Christmas Tree." He quietly stood inside the doorway, drinking in the amusing scene of the girl who "hated" Christmas flanked on either side with cooling cookies and a bowl of dough. His heart swelled, imagining a lifetime of Christmases with Liza. How great it would be to share his favorite holiday with his true love? He shook off the notion and came into the kitchen.

Liza spun around with a sweet smile, drying her hands on a towel, looking as pretty as always.

"You're home early."

"What's going on in here?" He slowly moved into the kitchen and popped a red-sprinkled cookie in his mouth.

"I thought maybe you'd like some Christmas cookies. I'm going to take a few dozen to the party tonight, too."

"So, Mrs. Claus *is* warming up to the holiday."

"Maybe" She pinched her fingers together with a playful wink. "Just a little. But really I just wanted to do something nice for you."

"Me? Why?"

"Because I didn't like how we left things last night. I felt really bad about the way I treated you."

He crossed the room, brushing crystals from his mouth while keeping her in his sight. He wanted more than anything to take her in his arms and kiss her properly, but last night she'd pushed him away and made it clear they couldn't cross the friendship line. Instead, he leaned against the sink, giving her a small nudge with his elbow, and a thumbs-up.

"Delicious. But you didn't have to do that."

"I didn't explain my feelings like I should have and after you told me you were there the night of the wreck, well, I—"

Her eyes welled and he could see she was struggling to get her point across. He grabbed the dish towel out of her hands and wrapped his arms around her. She burrowed into his chest and her warm breath seeped through his shirt.

"It's okay."

"I made the cookies because I know how much you love Christmas and I've been a big scrooge and I made you mad last night and I don't like it when things are awkward between us and you're my very best friend and no matter how frustrating and confusing and when you weren't here when I got up this morning and I'm sorry."

"Hey, take a breath. It's okay. You have nothing to be sorry for."

"Just because Christmas is a cursed time for me, I don't want to ruin it for you."

"You aren't cursed."

"Listen." She unlatched herself from his body and tilted her chin up. Dampness made her blue eyes sparkle and his heart skipped a beat. "I have so much I want to tell you and I promise I'll explain everything. But we have that dreadful Chamber of Commerce party at Diana and Bret's tonight, so it'll have to wait until we get home."

"It should be fun. We get to wear Santa costumes."

"Only you like wearing those goofy getups."

"Ho, ho, ho."

"Diana has let it be known that she has created a feast for tonight's mixer. I might not be much of a cook, but I dare her to top my amazing cookies. Can you believe they just moved into that house and already she's throwing a party?"

"She's quite a woman."

Liza held up a spatula, threatening to smack him with it. He should've known better than to praise Diana.

"Watch it, mister."

"Just kidding, just kidding." Tucker held up his hands in surrender and then snatched another cookie. What Liza didn't seem to recognize was she was way cooler than Diana, more interesting, more talented, and so much more beautiful. He never understood why she let Diana get under her skin. He would add that to his list of things to work on with her.

"So, other than baking cookies, how was your day?"

"Okay." She snatched oven mitts off the counter and reached into the oven. He admired her backside as she lifted another tray of cookies. "Just the usual, painting, baking, you know."

"That's good."

"Hey, have you heard about the castle in town? Did you know the city is selling it?"

"Sure, it's been in the paper."

"Did you know Bridges has submitted an offer and at least one other who plans to tear down the building?"

"Tear it down?" The sweet cookie turned sour in his mouth. Travis told him the other offer planned to restore the building. Did this mean there were now four offers on the building?

"Yes, isn't that terrible? I know whoever buys it will need to put in a lot of work, but it can't be torn down."

"I agree. I'll talk to Arthur about it if he's there tonight."

"Good idea. I'll talk to Virginia. I'm sure they would rather see the castle restored to its former glory. Don't you think that would be best?"

"Absolutely. Between the two of us, maybe we can convince the committee the castle's sale needs to go to the person who will save the building and make the best use of it."

"I couldn't agree more. Surely Mr. and Mrs. Claus carry some sort of clout, especially this time of year."

***

A hypnotic glow hovered over the landscape as if a flying saucer had landed two miles outside of town. Every inch of Diana and Bret's house was covered in miniature white lights while a spotlight illuminated an antique sleigh in the front yard. Liza was just glad they had arrived safely to this winter fairyland. The roads were a sheet of ice, putting her nerves on edge. Since the wreck, she avoided driving when the roads were icy, and was so thankful for Tucker's expert driving skills.

"It's a good thing there isn't an airport nearby." He maneuvered his truck between cars parked along the road. "The pilot might mistake this place for the runway."

"It looks likes Cinderella's castle was besieged by a pack of wild, light-bearing elves."

"But no princess lives here."

"Just the wicked witch of the west."

"Maybe we can throw water on her." He winked at her as he rolled into a spot in front of Brody's SUV. He cut the engine and then turned in his seat, taking her hand in his. "Now listen, Mrs. Claus, you need to be kind to our hostess. I expect you to be on your best behavior. No snarky comments. Be the good little lady I know you to be."

"I will, Mr. Claus. I promise. And even though he rubs you the wrong way, you need to be polite to our host." She smiled as she settled her white-gloved hand on his cheek. "Besides, nothing, not even Diana, can put me in a bad mood tonight. We're going to work our Christmas magic on Arthur and Virginia to be sure the deal goes to the person who plans to save the castle."

"I'm glad you're so supportive of the idea."

"I am. You have no idea how much I want to see the castle saved."

"Let's kiss on it for good luck."

"Good idea."

Pleasant warmth surged through her as Tucker cupped his gloved hands around her face and placed a delicate kiss on her lips. He had been so sweet when she had tried to explain in a roundabout way how sorry she was for abruptly stopping their make-out session last night. He hadn't pressured her about sleeping with him, or made her feel guilty about it, and had kept their friendship front and center.

Tonight, she would tell him about her injury and maybe then he'd understand why she'd thrown on the brakes last night. But as the days continued without a lightning strike or a natural disaster, and knowing Tucker was behind her idea to save the castle, she had started to think maybe the Curse of Christmases Past had lifted. Maybe it was safe for her to lower her guard and give in to her feelings for him, and maybe even share her secret. She wanted more of his mind-numbing kisses, to feel his hands on her again. Maybe there was a chance he'd accept her deformity and they could move beyond friendship to something lasting.

"Ready?" He asked with another peck.

"Ready as I'll ever be."

Diana met them at the door wearing a long, emerald, velvet gown trimmed in white crystals and a sprig of mistletoe in her hair. Since she couldn't be the official Mrs. Claus, she obviously had chosen to dress like her younger, hotter sister. Liza caught her own reflection in the foyer mirror and grimaced at her gray curly wig, wire-rimmed glasses, and muffin cap. It wasn't exactly her best look.

"You're here." Diana threw open her arms as if they'd just arrived home from a long night of toy delivery. "Look at you—so adorable in your Christmas finery."

Christmas finery? Maybe a space ship *had* landed on Diana's house and exchanged her for an alien life form from the eighteenth century.

As they stepped through the foyer, she and Tucker fell silent, mouths agape with wonder. If the outside of the house was over-the-top, it couldn't compare to the inside. The staircase was wrapped in fresh evergreen boughs and red satin ribbon. Fully-decorated Christmas trees adorned every room while festive music piped throughout the house. A cheery hum of conversation and laughter wafted toward them, shaking Liza out of her bedazzled stupor.

"Your house is beautiful, Diana. Really." Tucker should be proud of her sincere smile and kind compliment. The house was truly amazing.

"Oh, Lizard, thank you. We wanted it to be extra special tonight." Would she ever stop calling her Lizard? Liza took a deep breath while chanting inside her head, *I won't let her get to me. I won't let her get to me.*

"Thanks for hosting," Tucker said.

"We're thrilled to do it." With her hands clasped against her chest, Diana beamed with happiness. "Everyone who's anyone is here tonight. We have an epic turnout."

"Epic?"

Tucker answered Liza's question with a nudge to her ribs. She had promised to remain pleasant toward Diana and Bret, but epic?

"Yes, a huge crowd. It might have something to do with Bret and I hosting and Bridges Enterprises big plans for the castle."

"What happened to secret, sealed bids?" Liza asked as she handed Diana her cape.

"Oops, I guess I shouldn't have let that one slip." Her cousin's fake giggle grated on her nerves as she gathered Tucker's coat in her arms.

"The city hasn't decided on the fate of the castle yet." His harsh tone surprised her. Saving the castle really *was* a passion of his.

"True, but we all know they're almost guaranteed to get it."

"I wouldn't place any bets," he grumbled as he wrapped his arm around Liza's shoulders and led her into the party.

Any trepidation she had felt before coming was unnecessary. She knew almost everyone there and all were in a festive mood, and with Tucker's arm securely wrapped around her shoulder and his support of the castle, she felt invincible. After a while, they broke off on their own and she flitted from room to room, greeting all the business leaders of Highland Springs, while doing her duties without knocking over any decorations with her big, puffy dress. She found Virginia in the dining room with several ladies from the local garden club, discussing the unique arrangement of fresh mistletoe hanging over the table, tucked among the chandelier's crystals.

"It's quite a lovely idea, don't you think?" one of the women said.

"But it makes it tough to kiss under." Virginia's mischievous comment started a chain reaction of giggles through the group. "Well, if it isn't Mrs. Claus. How're you doing, honey?"

"Hello, Virginia, ladies. Sorry to interrupt."

"Oh, honey, you're not interrupting. Don't you look cute?"

"Thanks." Liza pulled a sprig of mistletoe from the chandelier and twirled it between her fingers, trying to decide the best way to bring up the castle project. She didn't want to be obvious in her inquiries nor lead Virginia to believe she was expecting any special favors. She just wanted to know what her chances were of securing the property.

"Where's that handsome man of yours?"

The mistletoe fell to the table as she glanced up at Virginia, flushed at the idea that Tucker was her man. "Tucker?"

"Of course, Tucker. You got yourself another handsome man I don't know about?"

"No, he's about all I can handle."

A collective chuckle rang out around the table. "That didn't come out right."

"Oh, honey, I think it came out just right." Virginia guffawed with a nudge to Liza's ribs. "I see the way he looks at you."

"What?"

"You can't fool me. He's had it bad for you for a long time. I'm just happy you finally let him catch you."

"Virginia, I think maybe you've misread—"

"Why do you think I nominated him for Mr. Claus? I knew the time was right. You must have picked up on it because, thanks to you, he finally got his wish."

"Oh…you mean his wish to be Mr. Claus, right. Since I agreed to be Mrs. Claus, he finally got to do what he's always wanted."

"I'm glad to hear it, honey, but he's been crazy in love with you what seems like forever."

Tucker was in love with her? The blood drained from her face as a thrumming warmed her heart. Was it just the romantic notions of an old lady or could Virginia know something Liza failed to see? No doubt a strong physical attraction was growing between them, but love? He kissed her like he meant it, and last night he wanted more, but he never said anything about love.

She looked through the doorway into the living room across the hall where he was deep in conversation with Arthur. He must have sensed her gaze because he lifted his head and gave her a quick wink before returning to his conversation. Kate had warned her they might fall in love while pretending to be a couple. The warmth spread from her heart to the tips of her fingers as she realized she was falling in love with him, too.

"Well, honey, I'm going to mosey into the next room. I'll see you—"

"Wait. I wanted to talk to you." She shook away the dreamy feelings and set her mind to the purpose of finding Virginia in the first place. "Can we talk privately for a minute?"

"Sure, honey."

They moved to a quiet corner of the dining room, leaving the garden club to argue over the ingredients in the artichoke dip.

"I wanted to ask you about the bids on the castle property."

"Now, you know I can't really discuss it. No decision has been made yet."

"I know, and I'd never expect you to tell me something that would get you in trouble. But can you at least tell me how many offers you've received?"

"Well…"

"Are the other bidders planning to tear it down?"

"I really—"

"Surely, the committee wouldn't allow that to happen. Think of the historical significance of the building. My great-grandfather built the castle and it can't be torn down."

"I thought you'd know about at least one of the other bids."

"I know all about Bridges Enterprises' plan to tear it down and build a gas station."

"Right, but—"

"And I heard about another plan to turn the block into retail space."

"Yes, but—"

"I also heard there is one other offer to restore the building, so that makes four. You know I want more than anything to win the bid and turn the building into an art gallery," she whispered just in case the ladies hovering over the food were listening, "but if the committee doesn't pick me, at least pick the person who plans to restore the building. More than anything I want to see it continue standing."

"Listen, honey," Virginia whispered, pulling her closer. "Rest assured I'll do everything I can to keep the castle standing right where it is."

"Thank you."

"I'm surprised you don't know the details of the other bid."

"Everyone in this town has been very secretive."

"Hmm. Well, I'll tell you this, but you didn't hear it from me. That other bid you mentioned…the plan is to keep the castle intact."

"It's good to know the castle has at least a fifty percent chance of standing."

"Odds are better than fifty percent, if you ask me." Virginia gave her another jab to the ribs and walked away, chuckling and shaking her head. Liza felt a wave of relief that at least Virginia planned to fight for the castle's survival, and her confidence meter went up several points knowing her plan was still in the running.

She glanced around. The dining room had grown quiet when the other women moved on with their plates mounded with finger foods. Liza was left alone.

So Virginia thought Tucker was in love with her. She glanced across the hallway toward the living room where he was still speaking with Arthur when a mischievous little thought prompted her to snatch another piece of mistletoe from the light fixture. She stuffed the greenery in her hand and walked toward the living room, hoping to get his attention. As she stood inside the doorway she looked him over, still focused on Arthur, his handsome face no longer hidden behind the fluffy beard, and wondered if the attraction she felt for him could be love. Lately, he was constantly on her mind and her thoughts were beyond those normal between friends. She had never even considered something more between them, but he looked so handsome. Even in his Santa suit, she wanted him in her arms now. But, if it was love, would he want her when he saw her scar? Even after eight years, it still made her cringe.

Tucker looked up and shot her a sexy smile. She lifted the mistletoe above her head and mouthed the words, "Back porch?"

FIFTEEN

Liza slipped down the hallway and through the back door into a room that had once been a back porch but had been turned into a sunroom. She shook her head in amazement. Diana and Bret had only moved in a couple of weeks ago and had managed to unpack as well as decorate every room in the house, including this one. Candles glowed in each window and garland hung along the sills. At the far end of the room was an antique washstand she remembered from her grandmother's house, now covered with framed pictures of family members past. She picked up a photo of her great-grandparents on her mother's side, looking for any resemblance to her, Diana, or Brody. This was the couple who bought the farm and built the house in which Brody and Kate lived now.

Along the opposite wall in front of a long row of windows sat a huge fish tank teeming with all sorts of colorful fish. Diana and Bret had even managed to turn the fish tank's lights red and green. She picked up a can of fish food and sprinkled a generous amount, smiling at the fish as they swam to the water's surface.

Ongoing chatter filtered through the walls, but she heard footsteps headed her way. She quickly set down the fish food and returned to the center of the room, closing her eyes and raising the green sprig over her head. The curse seemed to have lifted and Virginia's announcement made her decide to forget her vow of friendship. She was ready to explore the possibility they were falling in love. The door creaked open as Tucker entered the room.

"That was more than sixty seconds, I'll have you know." She giggled and puckered up, anxious for his heart-stopping kiss.

Instead of Tucker's soft, warm lips, she encountered cold, chapped lips, pressed firmly against hers. This mouth didn't feel like the one she'd been kissing lately. Still attached, she opened her eyes and found Bret nose-to-nose with her, eyes closed and cheeks flushed.

"What the hell?" Her powerful shove caused him to stumble into a hand-carved nativity scene.

"Hey, a cute lil' elf is waiting with her lips puckered? No way am I passing that up." Obviously drunk, Bret slurred his words and stalked toward her with his arms open wide.

"Stay back."

"Oh, come on, Liza, give me another kiss. I've wanned to do that since high school."

"You kissed me back in high school and then blew it." She picked up a flameless candle and waved it at him like a saber. "Don't come any closer."

"What do you mean? How did I blow it? You were the one who missed her chance."

"Best decision I ever made."

He tripped toward her, teetering side to side. If he came much closer, she would collide with the fish tank.

"Sure, that's right. Didn't wanna do it with a crowd watching."

"Among other things."

"We're alone now. Les pick up where we left off."

He lurched and yanked her into his arms so quick her muffin cap flew off and her wig went askew. A strong whiff of whiskey nearly took her breath away as he engulfed her mouth in an open kiss, jamming his tongue between her lips. She pushed again with all her strength, but he wouldn't release his hold.

"Liza!" Diana squealed.

"What the—?" Tucker's voice echoed against the windows.

She wiggled out of Bret's vise-like embrace and swiped the back of her hand across her mouth. Diana was standing in the doorway, hurt and fury etched across her face, and Tucker stood right behind her. Diana rushed across the room and grabbed Bret by the arm, dragging him around to face her.

"What's going on in here?"

"Let me splain." Bret's face had turned a ghostly white as he fought to stay erect.

"Liza, how could you?" Diana redirected her wrath. She shoved Bret aside and stepped menacingly close. "You little slut."

"What?" Those three words echoed through her mind, sparking a memory from the night of the wreck. Just as quickly, it was gone. "What did you call me?"

"Not satisfied with one man? You have to take mine?"

"He came on to me." She pointed at Bret who had taken several steps toward the door as if he planned to escape undetected. "I was expecting Tucker."

"But you settled for Bret."

"No."

"I knew you were faking. You and Tucker aren't really dating. You're just pretending so you could snatch the title away from us. And now you're trying to take my man away."

"That's ridicu—"

"Admit it. You'd do anything to stop me from getting what I want."

"I've never stopped you from getting what you want. Your life is golden."

"Oh, please, our whole lives you've tried to ruin things for me."

"Name one."

"The night of the wreck. Maybe it wouldn't have taken eight years for Bret and I to get together."

"Huh?"

"If you hadn't insisted we leave when we did things might have turned out differently."

Liza thought her head would explode. A throbbing pain started at the base of her neck and crept up toward her brain. It was so sharp she grabbed her head and doubled over. What was Diana talking about?

"Let's go, Liza." Tucker came into the room and slipped his arms around her, helping her to stand up.

"That's all you're going to say? Your *girlfriend* just made a pass at Bret."

"I didn't make a pass at him. It was the other way around." Bret slunk toward the door, eyes cast toward the floor. "Tell them, Bret."

"Come on." Tucker wrapped his hand around her shoulders and steered her toward the door.

"I was waiting in here for you. When I heard the door open, I closed my eyes and raised the sprig over my head." She did just that—reenacting the scene as it happened—while her brain pulsated. "Then this asshole kissed me."

"Is this true, Bret?" Diana asked the question like a school teacher questioning an unruly student.

"Tell her the truth." Liza glared at Bret, willing him to be a man and state the facts.

"Yes…" Bret gathered Diana in his arms. "Let me splain. I wanned to prove this *relazionship* is a scam. They're faking, like you said. The way she kissed me back proves it. Once a tease, always a tease."

"I should've known you were faking. Why would you do that to me, Lizard? You know how much we wanted to be Mr. and Mrs. Claus."

"For the love of God, would you stop calling me Lizard?" When Liza shouted in Diana's face, stars sparkled in her vision. A scene flashed in her mind, like a quick movie clip, of Diana in the backseat of a car with Bret. Was her memory from the night of the wreck coming back? If only she could remember everything.

She turned her attention to Bret, slumped against the doorframe. "I didn't kiss you back. Let's get that straight right now."

She then looked to Tucker who had said very little. "Tucker, you have to believe I didn't kiss him."

"Oh, please. You can stop the act. Always so dramatic." Diana forced her way between them and Bret, and looped her arm through his.

Liza turned into Tucker and tugged on his red velvet lapels. "It's not an act." The creases around his eyes and his furrowed brow sent a chill of fear down her spine. Had she held out her love for him so long that he believed she'd willingly kissed Bret? They may have entered into this under false pretenses, but there was nothing fake about her feelings for him now. She was sure of it. "Tucker?"

His lips curled into a wry grin and his gaze softened as he leveled her wig on her head, giving it a gentle pat before turning her around to face Diana and Bret. "I'm not exactly sure what the hell went on in here…" His arms enveloped her from behind and his cheek pressed to hers. "…but there's nothing artificial about the two of us except these costumes, isn't that right, babe?" He kissed her cheek and gave her padded waist a squeeze.

"That's right." Liza turned in his arms and pressed her thick, puffy dress into his heavy velvet coat. "Give me a kiss, Mr. Claus." She draped her arms around his neck and pulled him down for a slow, sultry kiss. Diana drew in an indignant breath. Catching Diana's outrage through the corner of her eye, she ran her hand down his back, letting it rest on his well-padded butt. Let her get a good look at their kiss—there was nothing fake about it.

After a long moment, he broke the kiss, keeping her tucked against him. "I'd suggest you get Bret a cup of coffee. Maybe once he sobers up you can get the truth out of him." He kissed her forehead just below her curly wig and said, "Oh and, Bret, just for the record, Liza has never turned me down. Must have been something about you."

"Oh." Diana huffed and marched out of the room, dragging Bret behind her.

"We better go, Mr. Claus. I think we've got some unfinished business back at the North Pole."

Liza winked at him through her wire-rims and slid her hand behind the buckle of his wide, black belt. The headache that had doubled her over had magically disappeared. His arms enveloped her and they laughed when he attempted to grab her bottom, only to get a handful of velvet instead. After a brief kiss, she looped her arm through his and led him from the room. They'd made it as far as the hallway when she remembered her hat.

"My cap. It fell off when that jerk kissed me." She hurried across the room and looked along the floor. Tucker joined in the search, finding her hat slowly sinking to the bottom of the fish tank.

"Do you think any of those fish bite?" He asked looking through the glass.

"It doesn't matter. I've got to get that hat."

"Let me find something to *fish* it out with."

"Very funny."

"I'll get some tongs from the kitchen."

"No need. I think I can—" she looked around for something to stand on, spotting a footstool across the room "—get it myself." She dragged the stool to the tank and climbed up, pulling her ruffled sleeve over her elbow. The water was warm against her skin as she plunged her hand into the tank.

"Watch out. That one looks hungry." The thought of a vicious fish sinking its tiny teeth into her hand made her lurch on the upholstered stool. Tucker rushed behind her and held her hips steady as she stood on tiptoe, reaching deep into the bottom of the tank.

"How's that?"

"Just a couple more inches."

He lifted her slightly, settling her bottom against his pelvis, giving her better reach into the tank.

"Better?"

"I'm almost there."

"You two are disgusting!" Diana had returned. With her loud shriek, Liza stumbled and water splashed over the side of the tank.

"I'm trying to get—"

"I see what you're trying to get off on." Diana stomped across the room and shoved Tucker aside. "First you kiss my boyfriend and then you let Tucker hump you from behind in my sunroom. Do you have any shame?"

"What are you talking about?"

"You. Bent over. Him. Thrusting behind you. You're sick."

"You can't be serious. I'm getting my—"

"And you had the nerve to call me a slut, a skank, and every other horrible word. Our mothers always wondered why we weren't close after the wreck, but out of respect I didn't tell them all the terrible things you said to me. It was your fault we wrecked that night. You ranting and spouting hateful words to me instead of watching the road."

The headache returned and her brain pulsed and throbbed as if it were trying to punch its way out of her skull. She spread her fingers over her scalp and squeezed, applying pressure to stop the pain. The thumping lessened and as it did a scene unfolded in her mind, and her heartbeat pounded in her chest. She remembered. A clear recollection of what happened that night opened up and she could see it all as if it were yesterday. Finally, the missing pieces of her memory were back in place.

Sixteen

Five days before Christmas, a bunch of high school kids and college guys home for winter break gathered for ice skating and a bonfire along the river. Beer, homemade moonshine, and hand-rolled blunts were being passed around. Bret kept eyeing Liza as she sat with her friends. He finally came around the bonfire and took her hand, leading her out onto the ice, slipping and sliding across the narrow part of the river to the bank where it was dark and secluded.

"I've really missed you since going away to school. I've always liked you, Liza. I think about you all the time."

She was floating on a cloud between the shot of apple pie moonshine and his lips kissing the side of her neck. She'd had a crush on Bret Bridges for over a year since they had that art class together.

"Even away at school, you're on my mind."

"I can't believe you think of me when you're surrounded by all those college girls."

"None of them compare to you."

Sitting side-by-side, he kissed her a few times, sweetly, but then more insistent. He rolled her beneath him and kissed her deeply, his tongue reaching toward her throat. He smelled of weed and tasted of moonshine, but in the brightness of the full moon, his eyes glowed like sapphires as he unzipped her wool jacket. With a quick jerk, he unsnapped his coat and tucked it around her.

"Don't worry, I'll keep you warm." He blew into his palm and slipped it under her thick sweater. Sweetly, gently, he caressed her flat belly, and she sighed against his cheek.

"You like that, huh?"

Yes, she liked it. She liked being there with him, kissing him. She answered by pulling him down for a long kiss. This had to be a dream. She was lying on the river bank, under a bright, full moon, making out with the hottest guy to ever graduate from Highland High, a boy who until last year had barely noticed her. Until now, she'd only made out with a couple of guys, and it had never gone further than kissing.

As if reading her mind, Bret reached behind her back and flicked open her bra strap. His soft, warm hand kneaded her breast and pinched her nipple. Her breath hitched as a hot, tingling sensation responded between her legs. So this was what it was like. She'd heard other girls talk about what they did with their boyfriends, but until now she had only imagined.

"Are you on the pill?" His question snapped her mind away from the pulsing in her body.

"What?"

"It's okay if you're not. I've got a condom."

"But, I—" He plunged his tongue deep in her mouth, halting her protest and popped the button on her jeans, snaking his hand inside her panties before she could stop him.

This was going too far. They hadn't seen each other or spoken since last summer. Shouldn't they go on a few dates, agree to date exclusively, take it slow?

He spread her legs apart with his knees and his finger slipped inside.

"You're so wet for me." He lifted her sweater and sucked her breast into his mouth. "They all said you wouldn't do it, but I knew you were a hot little piece."

Alarm bells went off. Her pulse thumped in her ears. He nipped at her breast and ground his bulging erection between her legs.

"Who said?"

"The guys."

"You've been talking about me to your friends?"

"Sure. You want it, don't you?"

"Bret, stop."

"Oh, no, I know you want me."

"Please stop. You have to stop." She pushed his head away from her breasts and yanked her sweater down over her nakedness.

"We're not stopping, you got that?" He pushed up on his elbow and unzipped his jeans. Even in the moonlit darkness, she could read his angry determination. While he pulled his pants down, she rolled out from under him and jumped to her feet.

"I've got to go." She reached behind and refastened her bra then zipped up her coat. "I'm, um, sorry, but I don't think we should."

"Shit, Liza, you can't leave me here with blue balls."

She wasn't quite sure what that was, but she wasn't ready for this, not this way.

"I like you a lot, Bret, I really do, but we need to take it slow. You know, maybe go out on a few dates while your home on break."

"Screw that. If you're not putting out, I'll find someone who will."

"But, wait, I—" What happened? He started out so sweet, and had even told her he liked her. He walked down the bank and started across the ice. "Bret, wait."

"Did you change your mind? Are we going to do it or not?"

This wasn't the way it was supposed to be. She'd always thought she'd make love for the first time with her husband or at least the man she loved and had a future with. She wasn't naïve, she knew lots of girls had already lost their virginity, but it had been with their boyfriends, right?

"I thought so. You're nothing but a dick tease."

Liza dropped to the river bank and sobbed into her hands. She'd had a crush on Bret for so long and wanted him to like her, but not that way. She couldn't just have sex with him, on the riverbank with everyone nearby, and not before they were a couple. He had rejoined his buddies around the fire. While passing around another joint, their laughter carried across the river and she knew they were talking about her. One of the guys pointed across the river at her and another peal of laughter rang out.

She wanted to go home, but she'd have to walk past the bonfire to get to her car. How humiliating would it be to listen to their heckles and jeers: "There goes Liza Fisk, little dick tease. Don't waste your time on her, guys." Dropping her head in her hands, she let another barrage of tears fall from her eyes.

Male voices carried from farther up the river and she saw a group of people skating in her direction. She recognized Tucker's voice in the group as it drew near.

"Lookie who we've got here. Is that you, Liza?" Tucker skated toward her and away from his friends. "What are you doing here all alone?" He came off the river, walked on blades across the frosty grass, and plopped down beside her.

"Where'd you come from?"

"There's a bunch of us skating below your house. We came down here to get a look at the bonfire. Make sure some idiots weren't trying to burn the forest down."

"There's a bunch of idiots over there, but they aren't trying to burn down the woods."

"Why aren't you across the river with them?"

"I don't want to be over there." She swiped her mittens across tear-soaked cheeks.

"Have you been crying? Come here, little one, tell ol' Tucker all about it." He wrapped his arms around her shoulders and pulled her to him.

"You wouldn't understand."

"Try me."

"It's Bret Bridges." Liza buried her face into his shoulder, drying the last of her tears on his coat.

"Asshole."

"We were skating and then we came over here and were—"

"Don't tell me you were making out with that creep."

"Things got out of hand."

"Did he hurt you? I'll break his neck." Tucker stood and started across the river. Liza went after him and grabbed his arm, stopping him.

"No, Tucker, stop. He didn't hurt me."

He spun around and gathered her shoulders in his hands.

"What did he do?"

"He wanted to, you know, go a little too far and when I told him no, he got mad."

"Good girl."

"No, you don't get it." She waved her arms toward the bonfire. "Now he's over there telling all his buddies I'm a dick tease and won't put out."

"Did he say that? I swear I'm going to crack that boy in two."

"Maybe he's right. Maybe I should have. I mean, I'm eighteen years old, a senior in high school. I'm probably the only girl who hasn't done it in my graduating class."

"That's not true."

"I'm sure it's true. Listen to them." She stomped her foot and a loud crack reverberated down the frozen river. "They're laughing at me and when I go back to school I'll be gossip fodder. It'll be all over that I turned down Bret Bridges. No girl in her right mind would turn him down."

"Why? That guy and his whole family are just rich assholes and they don't care about anyone else."

"You don't get it."

"I get it. Let me tell you something." He tipped up her chin, forcing her to look at him. "You did the right thing. Don't give it away to just anybody. You deserve a guy who treats you like a precious jewel."

"Oh my God, stop, Tucker." She couldn't listen to this corny stuff, but as she attempted to skate away, Tucker wrapped his hand around her arm, stopping her escape.

"It's true. You are funny and talented and smart and beautiful as hell. You don't need to have sex with that pervert to prove your worth in this town. You need a guy who will love you and cherish you."

"I think I'm going to puke."

"I'm serious. Listen to me." He gathered her face in his hands and leaned closer. "In a couple of years, when you're older, a great guy is going to sweep you off your feet and treat you like a queen."

"Oh, really, and you know this guy, do you?"

"Yeah, I do." He brushed his thumb across her cheek. "Me."

She wrenched out of his grip and glared at him.

"Are you drunk?"

"No, I'm completely sober, unlike that bunch of immature punks over there."

"Tucker, you're my brother's best friend. Ew, that's like incest or something." She scooted backward, away from Tucker who had obviously lost his mind.

"We're not related and, yeah, I'm your brother's best friend. What difference does that make?"

"You're like old. You're six years older than me. That's weird."

"But someday, you'll be older and it won't make as much difference."

"Ew, no. I could never date you, Tucker. That's just plain creepy. God, I've got to get out of here."

"Liza, don't go."

"No, Tucker, leave me alone. Don't ever suggest we go out again. That's just, ew, that's just wrong."

She pushed against his plump, protruding stomach and skated away. After crossing to the other side, she met up with her friends and told them she was leaving. Bret's friends were talking and laughing, and as she passed, they grew silent and watched her walk by.

"It's a damn shame she won't put out. She's hot."

"I'd do her."

"Maybe she just didn't want Bret. Hey, Liza, want to climb in my backseat?"

By the time she got to her car, hot, angry tears were streaming down her face, and she suddenly remembered Diana had ridden with her. She slammed her hand against the steering wheel, causing a numbing pain from her palm to her elbow. She climbed back out and went in search of her cousin.

She didn't have to go far before she heard familiar Minnie Mouse laughter coming from inside a car. She turned in a circle to find which car and her eyes landed on Bret's BMW. Diana's laughter rang out again and Liza knew she was in the car with him.

Liza pounded on the roof of his car and Bret opened the door. Diana was inside, topless with her pants unzipped, and Bret was furious.

"What the hell do you want?"

"Diana, I'm leaving. Bret can drive you home."

"Wait, Lizard. No. You have to take me home. My dad will kill me. Give me ten more minutes."

"No, I'm leaving now."

"Come on, give us a few more minutes," Bret said. Then he whispered, "It's the least you can do since you turned me down."

Without another word, Liza turned and stalked toward her car. Not only had he spread the news to his friends that she was a tease, but he had to go to her perfect cousin to get his thrills. Couldn't he have picked someone else? Of course, Diana had given him what he wanted.

Liza jumped back in the car, turned the ignition, and careened around several cars parked helter-skelter in the grassy field. She had just pulled onto the gravel lane when a hand pounded against the passenger-side window. It was Diana, still in the process of buttoning her coat. Liza stopped to let her in.

"What the hell is the matter with you, Lizard? You were just going to leave me? You couldn't wait ten minutes?"

"For what, so you can have sex with Bret Bridges?"

"Um, yeah. It's Bret Bridges. Nobody turns him down."

"So I've heard."

Liza floored it out of the holler. Her old Corolla struggled to climb the steep gravel road, its engine grinding as she pressed the gas pedal to the floor.

"You're such a bitch, you know that. I would've waited for you if the tables were turned."

"I wouldn't have been screwing in some guy's car."

"It wasn't some guy's car. It was Bret and it was a BMW. Who passes that up?"

"I did."

"Oh, wait…" Diana burst out laughing, slapping her hand against the dashboard. "That was you the guys were talking about? Oh my God."

"The very same."

"He said you wouldn't do it unless you were dating. You are so old fashioned. That's not how it's done."

"Obviously."

When they reached the top of the steep hill, the car skidded and swerved on a patch of ice-covered pavement. Liza was able to straighten the tires, but couldn't stop the flow of tears.

"You can't go to college a virgin. You can't. I mean everybody hooks up."

Rather than reply, she concentrated on keeping her watery focus on the road and the tires from slipping. A light drizzle fell, creating a thin sheet of ice on her windshield.

"Maybe I don't want to be like everyone else. What's wrong with waiting?"

"You'll die an old lady, a spinster. No guy wants a virgin anymore."

"Oh, really? They all want sluts like you."

"Did you just call me a slut?"

"Yes. How many guys have you been with?"

"More than you'll ever have."

"I'd rather die a virgin than catch a skanky disease."

"How dare you!"

Their voices were rising and Liza was having a harder time keeping her eyes on the road.

"Take me back. I'll find another way home." Diana reached for the steering wheel and Liza swerved, missing a tree by inches.

"Stop it. You almost made me wreck."

"It would serve you right. No one calls me a skank and gets away with it."

Diana reached over and yanked on Liza's coat. "You're such a bitch. You think you're so much better than me, but you're just a weirdo." Diana tugged back and forth on her coat, distracting her from driving.

"Let go, Diana."

"Not until you apologize."

"Get your hands off me, you little slut."

Diana punched Liza hard in the shoulder just as they were coming around a curve. The distraction caused Liza to spin on a patch of ice and swerve into the path of an oncoming pickup truck. The car spun three-sixty and crashed headfirst into an oak tree, and then tipped onto the driver's side. Everything went dark and Liza woke up five days later in the hospital.

SEVENTEEN

Liza's lungs ceased up, unable to breathe because of the memories flooding her mind. She doubled over and Tucker wrapped his arm around her waist, rushing her out of the house with waves of good-night as they hurried to his truck. The bitter cold helped expand her lungs and the pain surging through her head lessened. She stripped off her wig and glasses along the way, needing to get alone with Tucker. She had been so cruel to him that night. No wonder he held back his feelings for her. How could he even stand to be around her after the way she'd talked to him?

After helping her into the passenger seat, he climbed inside and she leaped into his lap, smothering his face against her shoulder.

"I'm so sorry, Tucker."

"What for?" His muffled response tickled the velvet against her skin and she realized she was suffocating him. She dropped back beside him and gathered his face in her mittened hands.

"For everything. Tonight I—"

"Forget about tonight. I knew it wasn't you. I'm just sorry Diana said those terrible things."

"No, that's just it. I'm glad she did. I remembered everything."

He drew back out of her grasp. The moonlight illuminated his wary gaze. "What do you mean?"

"I remembered everything that happened the night of the wreck—the parts I had forgotten. I remember Diana making out in Bret's car and the two of us fighting. I called her a slut and she punched me and grabbed the wheel and then headlights and then—"

Her heart was racing. Just saying the words made it all come back to her so vividly, she heard the screech of the tires and the blare of the oncoming pickup's horn.

Tucker cupped her face in his hands. "We don't have to talk about this right now."

"We do."

"No, we don't." His words were so emphatic, so final, he dropped his hands from her face and reached around her to start the truck. She scooted back to her seat and buckled up. He may not want to talk about it now, but when they got home, they would. She had to show him that was then but this was now. She was all grown up, knew what she wanted, and had indeed found a man who treated her like a precious jewel.

***

They rode in silence back to Liza's house, taking it slow over the icy roads. Tucker's concentration on getting them home safely helped control the rising panic seizing his lungs. If she remembered the details of the wreck, that meant she remembered her declaration that they would never have a future together. What if by remembering those words she would once again be turned off by him? She would think it was wrong to date her brother's best friend?

He followed her into the house and hung up their coats while Liza ran upstairs and slammed her bedroom door. Just as he suspected, those memories were doing a number on her and she wanted nothing to do with him. Maybe that was a good thing. He really wasn't ready to hear the words she had already tried to get through his thick skull: "We can only be friends."

Unbuckling the big, black belt, he dropped the Santa coat on a side chair and headed for the shower.

A half-hour later, he came into the kitchen to get a glass of water and found her sitting on the sofa in the soft glow of Christmas tree lights, wrapped in a satin robe.

"I thought you went to bed," he said, coming into the living room. Her face was freshly washed and her hair fell in soft waves down her back. With her legs tucked behind her, she shook her head and patted the cushion beside her.

"We need to talk."

The four worst words in the English language: *we need to talk.* How many break-ups, how many broken hearts had begun with *we need to talk*? He knew it was coming, so he might as well take his medicine and try not to choke on it. He sat beside her and put his glass on the coffee table.

"Tonight was crazy, huh?" She picked up his hand and held it in her lap.

"Crazy."

"And just to be clear, I didn't encourage Bret's kisses or ask him to do it or anything like that."

"Yup, I got it."

"But I did remember everything from the wreck, including the hateful things I said to you."

Here it came. They would forever remain just friends. She thought it then and had figured it still made sense now.

"Tucker, I'm so sorry."

He braced himself, prepared for the hammer to come down.

"I was so awful to you that night. If I could, I'd take it all back. I was a stupid teenager who didn't know what an amazing guy you were… and still are."

Wait, this didn't sound like the bomb drop he was expecting. She crawled over to him, rose onto her knees, and wrapped her arms around his neck.

"You said I was smart to wait for a great guy like you to come along, and I'm glad I did."

"You are?"

"You know…" Liza leaned in and grazed her lips across his cheek. "In case you were wondering…" She pecked soft kisses behind his ear. "I haven't been faking." Her tongue drew a wet line down his neck. "I tried to convince myself we should just be friends, but…" She stopped her tender assault and locked her eyes with his. "I don't think that's possible."

Happiness swelled in his chest. She was ready for more than just friendship. Things couldn't be more perfect than right at this moment. A flickering candle gave off the smell of fresh pine, the Christmas tree lights glowed softly, and the woman he loved was in his arms.

He ran his fingers through her hair, cupping the back of her head, and poured every blessed ounce of love into a kiss that brought a sweet sigh and her arms tighter around him. They stayed locked in the kiss while his hands explored the soft contours of her back and bottom. A moment ago he was ready to have his heart crushed and handed to him, but instead she was kissing him like her life depended on it. She straddled his lap with her pajama-clad legs and he rubbed his hands over her thighs and…

She stopped. Her arms dropped from around his neck and she scooted off his lap, tucking the robe tightly around her. What the hell happened?

***

"There's more I need to tell you before we, well…"

"What's wrong?"

How could she begin to explain about her leg, its ugliness, and how much she wanted to make love with him? What if he rejected her?

"Tell me what's bothering you? Did I do something wrong?"

"No." She turned toward him and draped an arm over his shoulder. "No, you haven't done anything wrong. It's me."

"Please don't start with that passionless, tease business."

"No, that's not it. I need to warn you of something, something few people know about."

They were sitting too close. His big, brown eyes were full of confusion. She needed space, some air between them. Popping off the sofa, she paced slowly in front of the fireplace, keeping her eyes on the flickering flame.

"My parents know, and Brody, of course, and Kate and Riley have seen it. It's so embarrassing and if I could I'd shield you from it but we're growing so close and obviously we're attracted to each other and eventually we're not going to be able to stop so I don't want you to be shocked when you—"

"Liza." She didn't even realize he had crossed the room and now his hands were cupping her face. "Tell me what it is."

There was no turning back now.

"You know my injuries from the wreck were—"

"A badly broken leg and head injury."

"Right, but what you don't know—haven't seen—is the damage to my leg."

"What do you mean?"

She took a deep breath, shook her head against the fear, and blurted, "My leg was mangled, not just broken, and I have a hideous scar that I'm afraid will totally gross you out."

The room turned deathly quiet and Tucker dropped his hands to her shoulders. She glanced up, catching his baseball-sized stare. That was it; he knew her truth and was shocked and disgusted. When she attempted to get away, he tightened his grip on her shoulders and threw his head back in loud, raucous laughter.

"It's not funny."

He continued laughing and anger swelled inside her.

"Stop laughing, you big oaf. It's horrible. It runs from my hip to my knee and it's all pinchy and jagged and...why are you still laughing?" She wrenched out of his hands and jabbed her elbow into his ribs before heading toward the stairs.

"Wait, wait, wait." He grabbed her arm just as she stepped onto the first tread. "I'm sorry, wait, I wasn't laughing at you."

"Well, if you weren't laughing at me, who were you laughing at?" She folded her arms over her chest and watched him struggle to wipe the smile from his face. How dare he laugh at her deformity? Did she make fun of him when he was overweight? Well, maybe she had, when she was thirteen, but this was completely different.

"I'm laughing—but not anymore—not about your injury. That's terrible for sure. But, Liza, do you think that matters to me? Babe..." He unfolded her arms, placed them on his shoulders, and pulled her into his embrace. "It wouldn't matter if you had an ugly scar running from your head to your toes, I'd still think you are beautiful."

"That's easy for you to say. You haven't seen it."

"Will you show me?"

Actually, she had hoped he'd never see it. When they finally made love, she planned to keep the lights off and the room in pitch darkness. Perhaps that was unrealistic. He needed to see it and determine for himself if it was something he could live with.

"Are you sure?"

"I'm sure." He lifted her off the step and pulled her by the hand back to the sofa. "Take off your pants and show me."

"Right here?"

"Yeah, right here. If you want, I'll close my eyes while you pull them down."

Tucker settled back against the cushions, crossed his arms, and closed his eyes. At least she was wearing a robe. She could open it like a flasher, give him a quick peek, and then wait for him to reject her. It would all be over in a matter of minutes.

She pushed her pajama pants to the floor and stepped out of them, leaving them lying in front of the fire. After adjusting her robe and tightening the sash, she walked over and stood in front of Tucker, her quivering knees threatened to buckle.

"Okay, you can open your eyes."

When he did, they immediately dropped to her legs and he leaned his elbows on his knees.

"I'm just going to open my robe enough so you can get a quick look and that's it. Okay?"

"Okay."

Her hands shook as she gathered the satin robe in her left hand and slowly pulled it up over her knee. Afraid to see his reaction, she kept her eyes on the task at hand, fighting to keep her breathing slow and steady. He didn't say a word as she raised the robe a little higher to expose the worst part of it where the injury had left a deep crevice in her flesh. He'd seen enough. She dropped the silky fabric from her hand and he grabbed the robe, pulling it open to expose her entire left leg.

"Tucker, no."

"Hush."

As light as a soft breeze, his fingers grazed along the scar, as if they were following the route on a road map. His eyes were hooded and his mouth set in a firm line. Why didn't he say something? How long would he make her endure this humiliation? She brushed his hand away and closed the robe, but he grabbed her wrist in one hand and pulled the garment away with the other. He touched his lips to the most hideous part of her scar and she jumped back, but just as quickly his arm snaked around her waist, stopping her escape.

"Please, Tucker, stop."

"Nope. Not stopping."

Her knees locked and she squeezed her eyes shut. She wanted to curl into a ball and hide when he began feather soft kisses down the length of her scar. How mortifying to have him so intimately close with his lips touching her awful deformity. She released the air from her lungs when he finally quit kissing her mangled leg. Instead of letting the robe drop, he pressed soft kisses on the other, unblemished thigh, and all at once her legs turned to jelly.

No longer frozen with fear, she melted to his touch and ran her fingers through his hair. This was nice. Her head tipped back and she sighed as he ran his hands up the back of her thighs. Palming her bottom, he let the robe fall back in place and smiled as he pulled her into his lap. She wrapped her arms around him and buried her face in his neck. He'd taken a horrifying moment and turned it into something beautiful. Letting out her pent-up breath, she snuggled in closer and laid her head on his shoulder.

"Thank you for not being repulsed." She chuckled and pressed a kiss to his cheek.

"No, I wasn't repulsed, but you weren't kidding. That scar is hideous."

"Tucker!" Tears filled her eyes and she attempted to push out of his arms, but she was no match for his strength. He forced her back onto his lap and held her head against his chest.

"Listen to me." Three sweet kisses grazed her forehead. "That scar is horrible, not because of what it looks like, but what you must have gone through to get it. I knew you spent a long time in the hospital, but thought it had something to do with your head."

"You had gone back to St. Louis, so there was no way you could've known. I swore Brody to secrecy. I didn't want anyone to know."

"What caused the scar?"

"My leg was ripped open from a piece of metal, but my head injury was a bigger issue, so it was close to a week before they could operate. I had two surgeries. With the first one, I had a reaction to the sutures, so they had to open it back up. Then an infection set in, so part of my leg had to be left open and heal from the inside out. That's what the crater is from. Plus, my leg was in traction so I have these ugly dimples on either side of my knee. It's a mess."

"So that's why you never want to come swim at my mom's house. I just thought you didn't want to see me in a bathing suit."

"I didn't want you to see *me* in a bathing suit."

They shared a laugh and then he smoothed her hair from her face, keeping his gaze locked on her lips as he leaned in. His kiss was sweet, loving and reassuring. Though it would always be an embarrassment, she was no longer self-conscious about her leg around him. He accepted her for who she was, including her oddly colored hair, lackluster career, and damaged leg. One out of the three would soon change—her dream of an art gallery was about to become reality. Maybe it was time to do something about her hair. That would have to wait. Right now, all she wanted was to be with Tucker and show him how much he meant to her.

After a few minutes of breathless kisses, she pulled back and climbed out of his embrace. She straddled her legs over his lap and raked her fingers down his chest and nuzzled his neck. While her nails drew circles at the base of his neck, she thought of the best way to tell him what she had in mind. After his tender acceptance of her ugly scar, there was nothing stopping them from being together.

She nibbled and pecked the length of his neck as her hands grazed down his muscular arms and slipped under his T-shirt.

"What are you doing?" His question came out ragged, from deep inside his throat. She grabbed the hem of his shirt and tugged it up and over his head, tossing it behind her.

Her lips brushed across the baby-fine hair on his chest. "I want you to do something for me."

EIGHTEEN

"Name it."

Right now, he'd walk across hot coals if she asked him. He felt like a wet noodle, totally helpless in her arms. The only part of him that wasn't limp with happiness, floating on a warm cloud of sexual pleasure, was the part that was straining the zipper of his jeans. Her hand glided across his pecs, raising his body temperature, and making the hairs on his chest stand on end. He slid his hand beneath her robe, inside her lacy panties, and with her soft cheeks fitted perfectly in his hands, he drew her tight against him. A moan escaped from deep inside his throat when she tickled his nipple with the tip of her tongue.

"I want you to make love to me."

She said it so quietly between kisses across his chest, he wasn't sure he'd heard her. He laid his hands on either side of her face and pulled her back so he could look at her. Her eyes were dazed with desire and her cheeks were flushed.

"What did you say?"

"I said." She crawled up his body and wrapped her arms around his neck. "Tonight is the night. You. Me. Tonight," she said between kisses placed on his nose, forehead, and cheeks. "It happens tonight."

"It does?"

She finished with a loud, final kiss to his breastbone and perched her elbows on his chest. "We're going upstairs to my bedroom and…" She brushed her finger along his clenched jaw. "Take care of business. Unless you don't want to."

"Hell yeah, I want to. But are you sure?"

"I've waited long enough and you're the only one I can imagine doing it with."

Standing her on her feet, Tucker jumped up then slipped his hands behind her back and knees. "As long as you're sure."

Cradling her in his arms, he surveyed the emotion playing on her face. Her heavy lids and tender smile, her hand fingering the fine hairs at the base of his throat spoke all he needed to know.

"Very sure."

***

Liza felt weightless in Tucker's strong arms as he effortlessly carried her up the stairs. His foot tapped her bedroom door closed and then he deposited her on the bed. She'd thought of this night for so long, never dreaming it would actually happen—and with Tucker of all people. The guy who had been her buddy, her pal, was now the guy she was falling in love with. They had jumped over the hurdle of her scarred leg, and she was determined to make the rest of the night memorable.

"Wait a minute." She popped off the bed and reached into her nightstand drawer for a votive candle, a book of matches, and a condom. "Just in case you're not prepared." She tossed the thin foil pouch to him and lit the candle, placing it on the nightstand. Every detail had to be considered for this momentous occasion. She had the hot guy, freshly washed sheets, and her legs had been waxed this morning. With the candlelight's glow and some soft music, she transformed her bedroom into a cozy love nest.

Tucker sat on the side of the bed, still shirtless and with a wry grin, looking so adorable and ready. She tapped a quick kiss on his lips. "I'll be right back." He'd have to hold on until she completed the last of preparations.

She scurried across the room to the bathroom, locking the door behind her, and dropped her back against it with a loud sigh. Tonight was the night. She was going to make love to Tucker—her first time—and surprisingly she wasn't afraid. She dropped her robe to the floor and stood in front of the mirror in only her cami and panties, turning left and right to survey her body one last time. If it weren't for her injured thigh, her body wouldn't be so bad. She had been blessed with her father's slim build and her mother's ample bust. For the first time in her life, she was ready to make love without pressure and on her terms.

She shimmied out of her panties and cami, and then pulled them back on again. Should she leave the robe on or off? Definitely on. She slipped her arms back into the sleeves and drew the sash into a bow. With a fluff of her hair, she was ready. As she reached for the doorknob, she decided it made no sense to wear anything under the robe. Maybe she should just strut to the bed naked. Her head thumped against the bathroom door and she drew air deep into her lungs.

"Are you okay in there?" It sounded like he was just on the other side of the door. If she didn't want him to come in after her, she'd better make a decision.

Undies off. Robe on.

With one final fortifying breath, she squared her shoulders and opened the bathroom door. He was again perched on the edge of the bed, just the way she had left him. He was so damned handsome. Why hadn't she noticed it years before? Her whole life he was just Tucker, her brother's best friend. The kid who seemed to always be at their house playing basketball with Brody or shooting cans with a BB gun in the backyard. He was Brody's college roommate, best man, and business partner—and, in the last couple of years, her closest friend. Who better than her best friend, the man she was falling in love with, to give herself to?

"Wow." His mouth curled into a seductive grin as he met her halfway to the bed. "It took you a little while. Are you okay?" His hands glided tenderly over the satin down her sides, over her hips, and rested on her bottom.

"I'm fine."

"You're beautiful. You know that?" His fingers gathered the silky fabric, bunching it at her back, and returned his hands to her bare bottom where he stroked her soft skin.

"So are you." She rose onto her toes and tugged his head down for a long kiss. It was strange; she wasn't nervous, not scared of the pain she might endure, just so ready to be with him.

He slid his arms around her waist and lifted her off the floor. Her hair draped around his face like a veil as they were locked in a kiss. He laid her down gently and leaned over her, bracing his hands on either side of her shoulders.

"Last chance. You're sure you want to do this?"

"Definitely."

"We can wait. There's no rush."

"I've waited long enough." She drew circles on his chest and then raked her fingers over his flat abs. He'd worked so hard to get fit in the last few months and all she could think about was him beside her in this bed. She wanted to make a special memory with Tucker.

"I just want you to be sure."

"Tucker James Callum." She sandwiched his face between her hands and tugged him down until their noses were touching. "If you don't get undressed and in this bed with me in the next ten seconds, you'll be sorry."

He dropped a quick kiss on her lips and burst out a chuckle. "Yes, ma'am."

Heeding her warning, he stripped down in less than ten seconds, his belt and jeans hitting the floor. She leaned up on her elbow and drew in a sharp breath as her eyes grazed over his delicious body. Appearing sheepish, he tilted his head and looked at her with hooded eyes.

"Well?"

"Three, two, one." She sat up and tugged him onto the bed. Then she rolled him onto his back, wiggled out of her robe, and stretched out along the length of his body with his face in her hands. "Are you ready?"

"The question is are *you* ready?" He gave her a tender smile and brushed his finger across the side of her face.

"Very ready."

"Well, okay then." In a flash, she was under him and his mouth covered hers. He kissed her slow, his tongue performing a sensuous dance, taking his time, and making her squirm with need. While one hand cradled the back of her head, the other slowly caressed her damaged thigh, trailing higher and higher, and instead of panic she floated. His fingers, long and slightly calloused, stroked a sensuous massage, sliding gradually to the soft flesh of her inner thighs. He was moving so excruciatingly slow, she thought she'd explode. He nuzzled the base of her neck, tickling her with kisses while his hand did amazing things below.

"Last chance to back out," he muttered against her shoulder.

"Nope. We're doing this."

And they did.

***

If Liza had known what all the fuss was about, maybe she would have insisted they have sex years ago. Drawing in a deep breath, she snuggled her face against Tucker's damp chest, drinking in his distinctive male scent, and sighed. It was the most satisfied, contented sigh she'd ever exhaled. Things had turned out exactly the way they were meant. There was a reason she'd never had sex before and it had nothing to do with her injury. She was meant to have it with Tucker and only Tucker, a man she trusted and who accepted her, quirks and all. Her arms tightened around him and she snuggled in closer, like a rabbit burrowing in for the winter. Her heart was so full she thought it would burst through her rib cage.

"You okay?" His warm breath stirred her hair. "Did I hurt you?"

Suddenly, her throat closed and she was unable to answer. Unexpected tears streamed from the corners of her eyes as she shook her head no.

"Hey." Rolling her onto her back, he rose onto his elbow and brushed his fingers through her hair. "I did, didn't I? I'm sorry."

Again, she shook her head, swallowing to ease the pressure in her throat. He'd been so gentle and now so sweet. She managed to answer with a faint whisper. "You didn't hurt me at all." She cupped his face in her hands and drew him down for a kiss. "You were very gentle."

"So, these are good tears?"

"The best." She nodded her head and wrapped her arms around his neck, pulling him into a tight embrace. "I'm so happy."

With a chuckle, he nestled his face into the base of her neck. "Damn, girl, you scared me." He pulled back and drilled her with a serious gaze. "I tried not to hurt you. I never want to hurt you."

She gave him a reassuring smile. "You didn't and you won't."

"That's a relief." Flopping onto his back, he stared up at the ceiling fan slowly stirring the air. He laid his hand on her thigh and turned his head to face her. "I wanted to go easy as possible for your first time, but I'm not sure I did. I'm sorry about that. It's hard to control myself with you."

"It was fine. You were great." She rolled over and planted herself flat on top of him. Her forehead rested against his as she dragged her fingers softly over his shoulders, down his arms, and across his chest. "But I was thinking, now that we got the dirty deed out of the way, we should do it again."

"We better wait until tomorrow."

Her forehead rocked back and forth over his as her hands slipped lower on his body. "Nope. I've waited twenty-six years for this and we're going to do it again and again. Unless you don't have the stamina, old man."

"Ha. Old man. I'll show you who's *not* an old man." As quick as an Olympic wrestler, he flipped her on her back, pinned her against the mattress, and gave in to her demands.

NINETEEN

The ceiling fan blew cool relief across Liza's bare skin with each tick-tick-tick of its rotation. The bed had grown warm and the sheets slightly damp. She wiggled her butt into Tucker's belly, snuggled into his arms, and muffled her giggles into the pillow when she found him once again aroused. They had made love twice more, each time surpassing the incredible fire of the time before.

"You awake?" His warm breath tickled her ear.

"Just barely." Gathering his arm against her chest, she exhaled a long, contented sigh.

"I've been thinking."

"Mm-hm." She closed her eyes, luxuriating in his large, strong arms.

"Now that we've made love…"

"Three times." She held up three fingers and pulled his large, strong hand to her mouth, Pressing tiny kisses on each finger, she marveled at how tender his manly hands could be.

"Proud of yourself, aren't you?"

"Very." She pivoted to face him and tucked her cheek against the downy hair of his chest. If only they could stay tangled up like this forever. "So, what were you thinking about?"

"Maybe I should move my stuff up here. Sleep with you every night."

"Definitely." Her lids were heavy, his spicy scent and deep voice lulling her to sleep.

"I knew it'd be perfect with us."

"Shh. Don't say that word."

"What? Perfect? It was."

Liza's eyes flew open, suddenly wide awake, and fear stabbed her heart as if jabbed with a cattle prod.

"You can't say that. We're already skating on thin ice as it is."

"What are you talking about?"

Wrapping the sheet around her naked breasts, she tucked her hair behind her ears and released a nervous breath. "Last night was great, beyond great. But you can't label this." She stirred her hands in the air. "Whatever this is, whatever we are, you can't use the P word. Just *thinking* the word could awaken the curse."

"Ah." He rolled onto his back and draped his arms over his eyes. "There is no curse."

"Whether there is or there isn't, we can't use that word. Say things are marvelous, incredible, fantabulous, anything but that word."

"You know you're crazy, don't you?"

"Every time my life was going great around this time of year, something bad happened. We are so good right now and I don't want to ruin it. Okay? Just keep your thoughts to yourself."

"Just to be clear, you remembered the wreck and Diana's role in it. Arguing with her and getting punched led to the crash. Plus, the roads were icy. It doesn't sound like a curse to me."

"Let's just avoid any reference to my life or our relationship as being per—exceptionally superb, just to be on the safe side. We might jinx it."

Tucker continued to lie with his eyes covered, shaking his head. Of course, she sounded a bit crazy, but the Christmas curse was real. Not all her bad Christmas memories were just small disappointments. The wreck had been a painful, life-changing event, and she didn't think she could handle the pain of losing Tucker if she really was cursed.

"Okay? You won't talk about feelings or our future or anything like that until around January fifteen. Agreed?"

"Fine," he grumbled as he turned to face her. "We won't talk about us as long as you agree there is officially an *us*."

"Yes, there is most definitely an us." She gathered his stubbled cheeks in her hands. "Now stop talking about it before a tornado hits the house."

"Okay, Dorothy."

"Okay." With a quick kiss, their pact was set and she burrowed into his arms once again.

***

This couldn't be happening, couldn't be real, but it was. Liza's face lay against his chest, her arm draped across his stomach, and Tucker thought his heart would explode with happiness. He wanted to tell her he loved her, but had just promised to keep his feelings to himself for fear it would jinx what was developing between them. At least she admitted they were officially an "us"—he could live with that for now.

"Hey, you never told me what you and Arthur talked about. Any news on the castle?" Her soft breath tickled his skin.

"He didn't give up much. Just said the committee would make their announcement at the Mistletoe Ball."

"But you were talking to him for so long. He didn't give you any hints?"

"Just that he felt the castle would be saved. Not good news for Bridges Enterprises."

But good news for him. Arthur all but confirmed the project was his. If the castle was to be saved it would be because he was awarded the bid. There was one other bid that proposed to save the castle, but the way Arthur had talked, he felt sure he'd soon unveil plans for his new pub. A smile spread across his face as he tucked Liza in closer. Everything was working out *perfectly*, so maybe it was time to let her in on his little secret.

"Virginia basically told me the same thing. She felt sure the castle would be saved and the bid awarded to someone who would best preserve the building and put it to good use."

"That's essentially what Arthur said."

"Which can only mean one thing."

"Yup, the winning bid will be—"

"Mine."

"What?" He nearly knocked her to the floor when he came off the bed. Had he heard her correctly?

"I submitted a bid to restore the building and use it as an art gallery. Isn't that exciting? You seem surprised."

He was having a heart attack. It was the only explanation for the tight clenching in his chest and the cold tingle down his back. He slapped his hands against his cheeks and rubbed fiercely, hoping to wake up from this nightmare. She couldn't have submitted a bid for the castle. That building was his. He'd sold his house and moved into a crappy camper to pay for the designs and renovations. He grabbed his chest, hoping to stop the arrhythmia.

She rose onto her knees and scooted to the edge of the bed where he stood. She rubbed the tip of her nose across his chest and he swallowed hard as she pecked a trail of tiny kisses over his throat. "Isn't it a great idea? An art gallery in Highland Springs?"

"Great."

"You don't like the idea?"

"Sure, um, I just didn't realize." When the hell did she come up with this idea? And why hadn't she told him? They seriously might have to call an ambulance. His heart was thumping erratically.

"I've wanted to open a gallery since I was a teenager."

"But in the castle?"

She slid off the bed, grabbing the comforter off the floor where it had fallen and wrapped it around herself like a toga.

"For the longest time, I didn't think it would be possible, but when I heard the city was going to sell the castle, I just knew it was the ideal place. Since it had been built by my great-grandfather it seemed meant to be that it would one day be back in the family." She shuffled across the room like a Geisha girl and spun around. "I've been saving every penny for the last few years so that when the right place came along, I'd have the money for a down payment."

"What about financing? And all the money it's going to take to fix it up?"

"I took a mortgage against the house."

"What house?"

"This house. I inherited it from Granny. I own one hundred percent of the equity so I was able to take out a substantial loan to cover most of my costs."

"But, babe, it's going to take a lot of work to fix up the castle. They don't call it Leaks-a-Lot for nothing."

"And Mice-a-Lot and Lost-a-Lot and Cracks-a-lot. I plan to restore it back to the days of Camelot Motors so that folks in this town can drop all those disparaging nicknames."

"Are you sure you can handle it?"

"Tucker, what's the matter with you?" Her eyes looked as though they'd come unglued from their sockets and he suddenly wanted to take back what he'd said. Of course, she could handle it. "I'm not stupid."

"Babe, come here." He stretched out his hand, but she slapped it away and took a step backward.

"No. Don't call me babe. Stop it. You don't think I can do this. You have no confidence in me."

"That's not what I meant."

"See, this is why I haven't told anyone. I expected my family to think I couldn't run a gallery, but I never dreamed you'd think the same thing."

"You are a strong, brilliant wo—"

"As I recall, you didn't know much about starting a business when you opened the brewery, but did I question your ability? Did I ask if you'd considered how much work it would be?"

"Liza, I'm sorry. Can we talk about this rationally?"

"Oh, so I'm irrational now? Just because I want to bring some culture to this town and create an environmentally-friendly green space?"

"Environmentally what?"

"Green space. A park. With a sculpture garden."

"Oh."

"Oh? That's all you can say?"

What he wanted to say was, "Oh, shit." He couldn't tell her that he was her biggest competition for the project. She was standing there, wrapped in that blue comforter, looking so damned beautiful and hopeful—well, right now she looked pissed—but her face had lit up when she talked about her gallery. Obviously, she'd dreamed about the gallery long before he thought of opening a pub. But he'd spent too much money on architectural drawings and site plans, he couldn't back out now. Maybe they could figure out a way to work together to make both their dreams a reality.

He stepped closer and reached toward her. "I'm sorry. Just caught off guard, that's all."

"I can do this and I will. That castle is mine; it's my gallery space. I'll prove to everyone in this town that I can be a success all on my own." She whipped around, away from his outstretched arms but her feet tangled in the comforter's bulk. She fell in a heap onto the hardwood with a heavy thump.

"Shit." He rushed over and helped her to her feet. "Are you okay?"

"Oh my God. Cover up."

"Why?"

"We can't talk about this with your…" She waved her hands like an orchestra conductor. "Stuff hanging out."

"Jesus. You can't be serious." They'd just spent the night together, completely naked and had made love three times by candlelight bright enough to see every private part of the human anatomy. He huffed like an angry bear and tugged the cotton sheet off the bed, draping it around his waist. "Better?"

"Much." Liza shuffled over to the vanity and, with as much grace as possible, plopped her bottom on the upholstered bench and gathered the excess comforter tightly around her. "I've done my research and already have several artists lined up for the grand opening. This is going to be a good thing for the town."

"I believe you. I'm sorry if I made you think I doubted you. But why didn't you tell me?"

"Because you know how it is around here. You tell one person and they tell another and before long the whole town knows your business and starts telling you you'll never make it work."

He raked his fingers across his scalp, giving his hair a painful tug. He remembered that feeling. When he had initially told a few people he planned to start a brewery, the first thing they asked was, "Do you know anything about brewing beer?" More than once his confidence had wavered, yet he stayed the course, making a few mistakes along the way, but ultimately creating a successful business. He had every confidence she could do the same.

"You'll make it work. I know you can do it."

"Thank you."

"Tell me more of your ideas." Maybe he could work a pub into her plans.

"I want to restore the castle to its original look, keeping the old woodwork, but putting in hardwood floors and new lighting. Outside, I want to create a sculpture garden, like I said, and put in benches so people can sit on a sunny afternoon or bring their dog for a walk."

"It sounds nice. Do you need the entire block to do that? Ever think of adding a few more buildings, you know, to rent out to generate more revenue?"

"No, I want the castle to be the centerpiece of the landscaped green space, with no other buildings to take away from its unique design."

"Okay, but you know the building is huge. Ever think of splitting it into maybe two spaces so you can rent out one?" He could easily put his pub in the back of the castle with access off the side street and maybe convince her to let him have a corner of the green space for a beer garden.

"I already have the plans drawn up the way I want it and it doesn't include rental space."

"But by renting out some space you could cover your expenses during the slower months."

"Well…" She tried to stand, but seemed to lose her balance in the comforter's weight, landing back on the bench. "That's not what I want, but I'll consider it."

"Listen." He gathered the bed sheets in his hand and bent on one knee, where he could look Liza squarely in the eyes. He unhinged her fingers from their death grip on the comforter and brought her hand to his lips. "Whatever you decide to do with the building, I know you'll be a success. As long as the committee doesn't choose Bridges Enterprises, your gallery will be a reality."

Her eyes welled with tears and his heart melted as he tenderly kissed her hand. At that moment, he'd give her anything she asked. Later today, he'd call the committee and withdraw his bid. Once it was awarded to Liza, he'd figure out a way to make both their dreams a reality—perhaps suggesting she rent some of the space to him for his pub. This plan seemed to help his erratic heartbeat and give him a sense of calm.

Liza squared her shoulders and looked him in the eye, sniffling back tears. "Thank you. I appreciate your faith in me. I might be jinxing it by saying this but with you by side, my gallery *will* happen."

"You've got that right."

TWENTY

At ten o'clock the next morning, Liza skirted the outer perimeter of the castle, visualizing the majestic building surrounded by lush, landscaped gardens. Tucker's suggestion to subdivide the building into rental space had at first offended her, but after further contemplation, she realized it was a smart business move. There were sure to be lean months, especially during the winter when tourism was low and the gallery wouldn't generate much money, so having consistent revenue from rental space made sense.

Across the back of the property was a narrow city street which could be the entry point for parking and the entrance to the rental space. She had studied the architectural drawings last night, penciling in a dividing wall across the back of the space with an outside entrance. She had originally planned to have her office in the back, but could easily move it to the upper floor, opening up room for a renter.

"Hey, girl. Fancy meeting you here." She nearly jumped out of her skin as she turned the corner to the back of the building and almost collided with Darla. "Taking another look?"

"Just doing some thinking. What are you doing here?"

"The committee asked me to provide some measurements on setbacks and easements. I was just going over my figures before I turned in my report."

"I heard they're making the announcement at the Mistletoe Ball."

"That's what they say. It just might be the highlight of the night—besides that special kiss under the mistletoe." Darla guffawed, causing her glasses to slip off the bridge of her nose. "Everyone looks forward to the moment Mr. and Mrs. Claus smooch. Sometimes a proposal happens." She wiggled her eyebrows at Liza with a playful grin.

"Not this year, Darla. Tucker and I are, well, we're not there yet." Since he'd moved into her room, the past few nights had felt like they were getting closer. Though he was passionate and called her babe, he hadn't shared what was in his heart. She had always loved Tucker, but that brotherly feeling had turned into something deeper, something that could last a lifetime. As soon as the holidays were over, she'd tell him how she felt, once the threat of the curse had passed, and hope he reciprocated that love.

"Well, you sure are a cute couple. It's nice to see how well you two are handling the competition."

"The competition?"

"Hang on." Darla held up her finger as her cell phone let out a shrill ring. She walked away, talking at lightning speed in unfamiliar real estate lingo. Wondering what Darla had meant by competition, Liza continued her trek around the building. The third and fourth bidders' identities had not been revealed, but she felt sure she would be awarded the bid. Bridges Enterprises were definitely part of the competition, but Bret had made it clear they would demolish the castle, which went against Virginia's wishes. As soon as Darla got off the phone, Liza would ask what she meant by competition.

"Hey, girl." Once again, Liza startled at Darla's sudden appearance. "I've got to run. One of my properties is in a bidding war."

"Oh, no, that doesn't sound good."

"It's great. The longer the bidding war goes, the higher the price, and the bigger commission for me." Darla giggled, holding her frames in place. "I'll see you tomorrow night at the ball."

"But, Darla."

"Got to run."

She was gone before Liza could ask what she meant by competition. She shook off her concerns, convinced she'd win the bid. Virginia and

Arthur were both behind the idea of restoring the castle. There was no way she could lose.

She stepped out onto the sidewalk, flipping the lapel of her wool coat around her ears as she walked back toward town. Snowflakes pebbled the air, swirling in the wind whipping off the mountains, the skies threatening to dump a few inches of snow overnight. Tomorrow was the Mistletoe Ball and it was setting up to be a winter wonderland, and a night she would never forget.

"Hey, babe, we've got to go," Tucker yelled up the stairs. "The ball will be over before we get there."

After three weeks of wearing the puffy red dress and gray wig to every event, Liza was happy she could go to the ball dressed in a formal gown of her choice. The owner of an art gallery needed to look the part, so this morning she made a trip to the salon for a manicure and new hair style, including a return to her natural honey blonde. No more blue, green or pink hair. It was time to look and feel like a successful business woman. She smiled at her reflection in the full-length mirror, thrilled with her newly layered hair cascading over the open back of her beaded midnight blue gown.

Tonight, she would surprise her friends and family when she was awarded the winning bid from the committee. Then she would meet Tucker under the mistletoe and give him a kiss this town wouldn't soon forget. It will be the start of her brand-new life, and nothing, not even the Christmas curse, would keep her from the happiness she deserved.

"Liza!"

"Coming." She took one last look with a deep breath, steeling herself for Tucker's reaction. He'd never seen her so, well, put together. Would he like the change? It was time to find out. She grabbed the silver clutch off her bed and squared her shoulders as she stepped through her bedroom door to the landing. He was waiting at the bottom of the staircase, adjusting the cufflinks of his tuxedo shirt. "Ready or not."

When he glanced up the staircase, his eyes bugged out and his mouth flapped open. She fought back a giggle as his Adam's apple bobbed with a hard swallow and his mouth gaped even wider. She milked her entrance, taking each step slowly, deliberately down the stairs. When she reached the bottom, she pressed a finger under his jaw to close his still-open mouth.

"Well?" she asked, tickling the soft flesh under his chin.

"Damn."

"That's all you have to say?" She laughed as his eyes trailed slowly from her face down the length of her dress and back up again, still big and round with surprise.

"Who the hell are you?"

"Tucker!"

"What happened to your hair? Where'd you get that dress?"

"You don't like it?" Threatening tears burned her eyes as his shock gradually turned to admiration.

"Liza, you look…"

And then to lust.

"Hot!"

"So, you *do* like it?"

"Babe, you're gorgeous, beyond gorgeous. Shit, I don't even know how to tell you how good you look. Too damned beautiful to be seen with me."

"Stop it. Let me look at you. So handsome in your tux. Turn around."

"No, you turn around."

She obliged, tip-toeing in a circle, while he let out a long, slow whistle.

"Let's forget the ball and go back upstairs." He pulled her into his arms and assaulted her neck with wet, warm kisses.

"Nope, you have to take me out first."

"You sure about that?" His warm breath brushed her skin as he skimmed his lips behind her ear and across her cheek until he captured her mouth. She gave into his passion for a few seconds, enjoying the tingle his lips created, but she couldn't let him go any farther for fear her nether regions would take control of her brain.

"Positive." She managed to squeeze her hands between them and push against his chest, sending him stumbling against the wall. "Behave yourself for the next couple of hours and I'll let you carry out whatever fantasy you have swirling in your mind when we get home."

"I'm not sure I can last that long."

"You'll have to. It's your last duty as Mr. Claus and I have to look presentable when they announce my winning castle proposal."

"You're still convinced you've got this."

"Yes. For the first time in years, I don't feel the Christmas curse hanging over me. Having you in my life seems to have warded off the evil spirits."

"Good, because I have something for you." His lips curled into a boyish grin as he slipped his hand inside his tuxedo jacket.

What in the world could he have hidden in his pocket? A quiver wiggled down her spine as his hooded gaze stayed locked on hers. He was definitely up to something with that wry grin and flushed cheeks. It was something important and the wait was killing her. Was he about to propose? They'd been officially *us* for such a short time, wasn't he jumping the gun? On the other hand, they'd been inseparable for nearly two years; it wasn't like they were still getting to know each other. That had to be it. He was going to propose. She pressed her fingers to her tear ducts preparing for the big question.

"This is for you."

Instead of a little velvet box, he held a shiny brass skeleton key in his hand, tied with a red satin bow. Her heart sank to her stomach and her face grew hot. How silly she was to hope for an engagement ring.

"What is it?"

"It represents two things. One, I'll tell you now, and the other will have to wait until we get to the ball."

"Okay...what's the first one."

"This, my angel..." He wrapped his arm around her waist and pulled her close while he dangled the key in front of her face. "...represents the key to my heart. It's yours now and forever."

"Oh, Tucker." It wasn't a marriage proposal, but it was very close. More than that, though he hadn't said the words, it proved that he loved her. His feelings ran much deeper than just friendship. She lifted the key from his fingers and kissed it before smothering it in her hand. "That was so sweet. Thank you. And you have my heart, too."

He kissed the hand holding the key and tugged her closer. "I guess you better keep me around until next Christmas." He brushed his lips across hers.

"And the Christmas after that." She slipped her arms around his neck, rising taller in her heels, and kissed him tenderly.

"And the next Christmas." His tongue prompted her lips open.

"And the next." Her tongue tangled with his as they fell against the wall, kissing as if they had nowhere to go.

TWENTY-ONE

"Thirty minutes late isn't so bad, is it?" Liza asked, clenching her bottom lip between her teeth, as they entered the hotel ballroom to rousing applause. The band had stopped their song for a high-speed drum roll ending with a crash of the cymbals.

"Ladies and gentleman, Mr. and Mrs. Claus have arrived," Arthur announced through the stage microphone, "looking a bit different than the last time we saw them. Let the party begin!"

Arthur signaled them to the center of the room as the band began "White Christmas," the traditional first dance of the Christmas couple at the Mistletoe Ball. For several minutes, the crowd circled the dance floor, watching as Tucker and Liza swayed to the music.

"Everyone's watching you," he sang in her ear.

"And you."

"No way, not with you in that dress."

She grazed her fingers inside the collar of his crisp white shirt, tickling the back of his neck. She had never dreamed she'd be in his arms, falling deeper and deeper in love in the middle of the dance floor under the enormous ball of mistletoe where later they would have their official kiss. Maybe Christmas wasn't cursed after all. She had the key—her new lucky charm—tucked inside her clutch, and knew that nothing or no one could ruin this night. Right now, with Tucker's strong hands splayed against her bare back, she felt fearless, confident, and convinced she was the luckiest girl in the world.

Several songs later, they wandered toward the bar, greeting guests as they passed. Kate and Brody were seated at a table with Virginia and Arthur. Virginia rose from her seat and gave them each a big hug.

"Don't you two look splendid? I love your hair, honey. Sure beats those crazy colors."

"Gram!" Kate rushed to Virginia's side and grabbed her elbow.

"You know it's true. Liza's too darned pretty to have pink hair."

"Gram, you really shouldn't—"

"It's okay, Virginia. I appreciate your honesty."

"Brody and I are going to the bar. What can I get you?" Tucker asked, slipping his arm around Liza's waist.

"White wine."

"You got it." He patted her beaded bottom and followed Brody across the room.

"Are you enjoying your big night?" Kate asked.

"Absolutely. I never thought I'd say that."

"See, I knew you and Tucker would have a good time being Mr. and Mrs. Claus. That's why I nominated him," Virginia said.

"Who would have guessed he'd pick the girl who hates Christmas to be Mrs. Claus?" Kate chuckled, tipping her wine glass to her lips.

"I'm warming up to the holiday after all."

"And warming up to Tucker?"

"You could say that."

"Are you ready for the big announcement later?" Virginia glanced over her glasses frames, her brows arched and a playful grin on her face. "I think you'll be surprised."

"Surprised?" Liza's heart dropped. She didn't like that word *surprised*. "I'm hoping to hear the committee say the castle will be saved." And her name attached to the winning bid.

"I don't think you have anything to worry about, honey. Arthur and I made sure that old building will continue to stand."

"So, are you telling me…?"

"I'm not telling you anything. I'm sworn to secrecy." Virginia drew a cross over her heart and her finger across her lips. "I just can't wait to see your reaction, that's all."

"Jeez, Gram, why don't you go ahead and tell us already?"

"Nope, you couldn't pry it out of me."

"Couldn't pry what out of you?" Diana had zoomed in like a stealth bomber and joined the conversation. "Is there a big secret you're dying to spill?"

"Hello, Diana." Virginia squeezed her hand while Kate and Liza stood silently. "Don't you look nice?"

"Thank you, Virginia. It's couture."

"It's what?"

"Couture. Designer, one of a kind."

"Oh, I've heard of that. They don't sell that around here."

"Of course not. I bought it in New York."

"Seems like a long way to travel just to buy a dress."

"I wanted something unique. Something you don't see everywhere." Diana's artificial lashes blinked rapidly as she cast a glance down the length of Liza's gown. She never failed to find a way to put Liza down, but even her snide remarks couldn't ruin the night.

"Well, my dress came from JC Penney and it's just fine by me." Virginia ran her hands over her hips and gave Kate and Liza a conspiring wink. "I think I'll get myself a plate. Talk to you girls later."

Virginia shuffled away and Liza started to follow, but Diana laid her hand on her arm, stopping her escape.

"I guess I walked up too soon. It sounded like Virginia was about to tell you who won the bid on the castle."

"No, she swore she wouldn't tell anyone," Kate said.

"Well, it doesn't matter. Bridges Enterprises lost out, so I hear. The narrow-minded committee wanted to save the castle for historical reasons even though everyone can see it's a monstrosity."

"How do you know Bridges lost out?" Liza asked, trying to contain her excitement. If they were officially eliminated, that improved her odds dramatically.

"Someone on the committee—I'm not naming names—gave Bret a call this morning, giving him a heads-up. He didn't want him to be humiliated in public with the announcement."

"That was very considerate of this mysterious member." Kate leaned closer to Diana and spoke just above a whisper. "Did they say who may have won?"

"Only that it was between Tucker and Liza."

"Tuck—what?" Liza's stomach sank to her knees. Surely Diana was mistaken.

"You and Tucker were the only other bids and both wanted to save the castle."

"You put in a bid for the castle?" Kate's reaction was one of surprise rather than shock. "That's where you're putting your gallery?"

"That's the plan but, Diana, I think you got your information wrong." Liza's throat tightened as her chest clenched with fear. Tucker hadn't bid on the property. Surely, he would have told her as many times as they'd discussed it lately. He knew it was her dream location for the gallery. He wouldn't bid against her.

"Oh, I've got the right information. Tucker wants to put in a pub and build a bunch of stores on the lot, like a retail plaza. I overheard him talking with Arthur about it at our Christmas party."

"Tucker wouldn't do that. He would have told me."

"Uh oh, is there trouble in paradise? Your boyfriend keeping secrets?"

"Shut up, Diana. Kate?" Liza's eyes darted to her sister-in-law, hoping she would see doubt and confusion, but her face was tipped to the floor, her expression hidden behind her flowing hair. "Do you know anything about this?"

Kate raised her head, sadness etched across her face. "No, I don't. I swear. I'm just so surprised. Tucker wants to start a pub and you want to open your gallery? If this is true, Liza…I'm so sorry."

"Do you think it's true? He wants to put up a bunch of buildings and turn the castle into a bar?"

"According to our source…" Leaning close, Diana spoke in a stage whisper. "It's not your run-of-the-mill bar, but a really nice pub. It's supposed to be just like you'd find in England."

"Oh my God, and he didn't even tell me."

"Well, well, well. The so-called *relationship* of yours seems to have run aground. I guess it's not going to be a very Merry Christmas for you." Diana sashayed away with a shrill laugh, clearly proud she'd given Liza the shock of her life. The pain in Liza's chest made her double over. She pressed her fist into her diaphragm and concentrated on taking slow, steady breaths. The curse of Christmas had returned, putting a halt to her happiness. When the pressure subsided, she stood up straight and looked around the ballroom for Tucker. She found him standing near the bar, deep in conversation with Travis and Brody, a content smile on his face. How could he have kept this from her?

Her gaze then landed on Diana, whose hands waved in the air as she told a story to a group of Highland Springs' "who's who," satisfaction and pleasure sparkling in her eyes. Once again, her Christmas—no her happiness—was ruined. She was so sure the curse had lifted. The key, and the love she felt for Tucker and from him, would protect her from anything bad happening.

Her eyes drifted back to Tucker, who caught her stare and blew her a kiss followed by a wink. How could he play the sexy boyfriend knowing he'd kept this from her? When she looked again at Diana, she received a smug, wry grin and a nonchalant shrug of her shoulders. How many times had she seen that gesture before? Their whole lives, Diana seemed to celebrate whenever something bad happened to Liza. Well, she could swim around in her pool of satisfaction. She couldn't be bothered with Diana's reaction. She needed to focus on Tucker and why he had done this to her.

"I need some air." She wobbled around toward the door.

"I'll come with you," Kate said.

"No, that's okay. You stay. I just need to get out of here." On unsteady legs, she rushed toward the door, weaving between gyrating bodies on the dance floor. She had just cleared the crowd when Tucker stepped in front of her.

"Babe, where are you going?"

"Outside."

"It's like zero degrees out there. I'll go with you. You can wear my jacket."

"No." She turned around to face him, whose sweet smile seared her heart. He had known about her gallery plans for over a week and hadn't bothered to confess that he too had submitted a bid. He'd never kept secrets from her before. "Why didn't you tell me?"

"Tell you what?"

"Come on, Tucker. I know all about your plans to turn the castle into a pub."

His face turned pale white and he swallowed deeply. When was he planning to tell her? After he was awarded the bid?

"Well?" She crossed her arms and glared, willing him to man-up.

"How did you find out?"

"Diana. Who else? She couldn't wait to gloat over another failed Christmas."

"It's not a failed Christmas. We're having a great time."

"You may be, but I just found out the man I love has been keeping secrets and trying to undermine my plans for an art gallery."

"The man you—"

"You know what that building means to me. I've shown you the drawings, explained the layout of the sculpture garden. All this time you didn't bother to tell me you wanted to cover the entire block with retail space and open a pub."

"It's not like that." He gathered her shoulders in his hands and bent down to her eye level. "Let's get back to the part about how you love me."

"Tucker! Oh my God. I'm talking about trust or the lack of it. I trusted—"

"Ladies and gentleman, may I have your attention?" Her tirade was cut off when Arthur's voice came over the microphone. "Is everyone having a good time?" The crowd responded with a hearty cheer.

"Before we have the traditional kiss under the mistletoe, I'd like to make a special announcement. As you all know, the mayor appointed a committee to review plans for the abandoned castle and award the winning proposal tonight at the ball. It's sort of a Christmas gift to the town."

"I don't think I can listen to this." She turned toward the door, but Tucker wrapped his arm around her shoulders, forcing her to stay.

"We had three interesting proposals, each with their own merits. But the committee felt it important to save the historical building, which has sat on that corner since the early nineteen hundreds. We also wanted to see the entire block put to good use, generate needed tax dollars, and enhance the appearance of our downtown."

"Tucker, let me go."

"No, you have to hear this."

"It is with great pride I announce the unanimous decision that the project be awarded to Tucker Callum…" As the ballroom erupted in applause, Liza thought she would be sick. Her stomach roiled as her dream of an art gallery inside the castle was crushed by the man she thought she loved. As if in a trance, she struggled out of his grasp and slogged toward the door.

"…and Liza Fisk for their proposal to turn the castle into an art gallery."

She halted her escape. A cold shiver coursed down her spine. Had she heard Arthur right?

"Take a look at the screen behind me. This is the architect's rendering of the winning proposal."

She heard the whir of a motor and turned to see a large, white screen descend from the ceiling. A photograph of the castle appeared on the screen with a sign over the double doors *The Fisk Gallery*. In the foreground and on one side of the building were landscaped areas adorned with Roman and modern sculptures, almost identical to her drawings.

"Now, on the east side of the lot, Tucker and Liza plan to build a traditional English pub with a beer garden open during the summer months, along with four additional retail spaces." Arthur clicked the remote and the image changed to a central Tudor building flanked on both sides with additional stores in the same architectural style.

"What do you think, folks?"

Applause and whistles echoed off the ballroom walls as her fisted hands turned numb. She looked at Tucker, still standing near the door, with his hands stuffed in his pockets, looking a bit sheepish, but with a wide, proud grin on his face. Did he think just because the castle had the Fisk Gallery plastered over the doorway, that she could forgive his deceit? For the past six days, he hadn't bothered to tell her he had bid on the building and now he assumed his fancy drawings would be acceptable to her? The night she told him about the gallery he asked if she could handle it. Obviously, he didn't think so or he wouldn't have had these plans drawn. She wanted and needed to do this on her own, but he had taken the chance away from her because he doubted she could *handle* it.

"Well? What do you think?" He ran his hands down her arms and gathered her hands in his. "You and me? Partners in the castle project?"

"Tucker, this was my gallery, my dream."

"I thought you'd be happy. That's what the key represented. Our business partnership."

A business partner? What an idiot she was to think he loved her and was planning to propose. That key wasn't the key to his heart; it was for his stupid pub—which he had kept secret—and his ambush of her castle.

"It was supposed to be my project. I mortgaged my house."

"Well, I sold mine and moved into a camper. You're not the only one who has sacrificed for this project. I did this for you."

"You didn't do this for me." She shook out of his grasp and pulled the key from her clutch. "Take your key. We're not business partners. You and me, whatever we are—were—it's over."

TWENTY-TWO

The doorbell wouldn't stop ringing. Liza squeezed her head between two pillows and curled up like a shrimp. When would he get the hint she didn't want to see him or talk to him? Every hour, on the hour, she received a text or a phone call, and twice he'd pounded on her door. She had stuffed his clothes into a box and set it on her porch, so there was no reason for Tucker to be here. The shrill tone penetrated through the stuffing, jangling her nerves. Why wouldn't he stop?

"Go away, Tucker!"

The ringing stopped and a fist pounded on the door. No, it was two fists.

"Open up, Liza. We know you're in there."

Kate was at her door and she wasn't alone. Liza really wasn't in the mood to listen to her brother tell her what a big baby she was being. But, if she didn't answer the door, they would never go away. She dropped the pillows to the floor and tugged her slippers on. As she shuffled to the door, a painful twinge shot through her lower back. She ached all over from too many hours spent on the couch. Sleeping alone in her bed brought back heartbreaking memories.

"It's about time." Kate barked as she and Riley huddled on her porch, shivering. "I should've brought my key. I didn't expect you to leave us out here to freeze."

"Sorry. I thought it was Tucker."

She shuffled back to the sofa and curled up in the corner, pulling a cotton throw over her shoulders.

"Gram sent us to stage an intervention."

Kate plopped beside her and Riley sat on the coffee table. They had her cornered and she didn't have any choice but to listen.

"Where's Brody?"

"Down at the house. He says he's staying out of it."

"Coward."

"It's been two days." Riley laid her hand on Liza's shoulder. "You can't stay holed up here in your pajamas."

"Got a better idea?"

"Yes, you need to talk to Tucker."

"Gram says the committee is waiting for you to sign the papers so the project can move forward."

"Tucker can have it."

"You don't mean that," Riley said. "What about your dream?"

"Dreams aren't reality. Obviously, Tucker didn't think I could make a success of the gallery. Maybe he's right. What do I know about running a gallery? I guess the committee thought it would be cute to award the bid to Mr. and Mrs. Claus."

"I'm sure there's more to it than that," Kate said. "When was the last time you ate or took a shower?"

"What difference does it make?" She slumped down into the sofa and pulled the throw over her head. "I'm never leaving my house again."

"Stop being such a drama queen." Kate yanked off the throw and tossed it to the floor. "What happened to my feisty, outspoken sister-in-law? The one that fought back from a terrible accident, finished college in three years, and started a successful online card business? Since when do you let a little setback get in your way?"

"Since my short-lived boyfriend stabbed me in the back."

"Come on, you're coming with us." Riley ripped the pillow from beneath her head and forced her to sit up. "You're going down to city hall and demand they turn the property over to you alone."

"Right, show them you are more than capable of turning that castle into Camelot again." Kate shoved her hands into Liza's armpits and lifted her to her feet. "You've got one hour to get showered and dressed. We'll give you a ride to town since it snowed overnight."

If her two best friends had this kind of confidence in her, then maybe she should demand the committee give her the bid. At the very least, she deserved an explanation as to why she and Tucker had been awarded it together. Was it some publicity stunt on the part of the committee or had Tucker wrangled them into the decision because he didn't think her gallery would survive?

"I don't need an hour. I'll be ready before you blink."

***

"Are you sure this is what you want to do, Tucker?"

Arthur sat at the head of the conference room table with the other four members of the committee on either side. Liza wouldn't take his calls, wouldn't open her door to him. She obviously didn't want to be in business with him or want to know why they won the castle bid. What hurt the most was when she said they were through. He didn't need to own a pub. He had a successful business already. And in a few months, he could save up enough money for a down payment on another house, move out of the camper, and maybe by then she would be ready to forgive him.

"Yes, I'm sure. I'm withdrawing my bid. Give it to Liza."

"Well now, that's where we run into a little snag," Arthur said, rubbing the stress lines on his forehead. "As you recall, when you approached us about combining your bids, we told you we—"

Arthur was interrupted when the conference room door flew open and Liza marched in. Her ponytail wagged behind her as she looked around the room, glancing at each of the committee members until her gaze locked on Tucker. Her furrowed brows and pursed lips sent a shiver through his limbs. She was still furious at him.

"I'd like a moment to address the committee, please." She stalked around the table and took a seat between Virginia and Sam Smiley, the local funeral director. If she had her way, Tucker would be Sam's next customer.

"Go right ahead, Liza. What's on your mind?" Arthur slipped Tucker's withdrawal letter into a file as everyone turned their attention to her.

"I apologize for my abrupt departure from the ball the other evening. But, as you've probably been told…" Tucker slumped lower in his seat when she glared at him. "…I was not aware that Tucker Callum had submitted a bid, let alone talked you into combining our ideas."

"He didn't exactly talk us into it, honey." Virginia's gentle pat on her hand didn't seem to squelch Liza's fire.

"That castle was built by my great-grandfather and has stood on the corner of Main Street and College Avenue for almost one hundred years. Highland Springs is a growing community and would welcome and support a cultural experience such as my art gallery. My business plan is solid, based on a great deal of research, and I feel confident I will easily reach my financial goals. You can rest assured, under my ownership the castle will never again sit abandoned."

Damn, she was beautiful when she was fired up. There was no question she would make a success of the gallery with such drive and determination. Her business model and renovation plans were expertly crafted, and her connections in the art community would draw in the biggest artists from all over the country. Her gallery was a surefire winner. But if her stubborn pride would have let him explain, she would have known there was more than just restoring the castle behind the committee's decision.

"Perhaps we should explain how we came to our decision." Arthur pushed up his glasses and clasped his hands on the wood table.

"Thank you. I would appreciate that."

"A few days before the ball, Tucker asked for a private meeting with the committee. This, of course, went against our protocol for secret, sealed bids. None of the bidders were to know about the other bids. But, since you had told Tucker about your bid, we decided to sidestep our protocols and listen to what he had to say."

"Which was?" Liza tipped up her chin, puffed out her chest, and crossed her arms. There was no doubt she thought he had double-crossed her.

"Tucker came to withdrawal his bid. He didn't want to compete with yours."

Instead of looking at him with a grateful smile, Liza tossed her hair over one shoulder and raised her chin up a notch.

"We told Tucker that the committee was on the fence because we absolutely wanted to save the castle, but the amount of tax revenue and employment opportunity Bridge's convenience store would bring was hard to pass up. From an aesthetic, cultural standpoint, we liked your gallery idea the best. Then, on the other hand, Tucker's idea would have extended the downtown commercial district and increased property values."

Was any of this sinking in with her? She still had the defiant, distrustful look on her face. Surely, she could appreciate the difficult position the committee was in.

"After Tucker left, the committee met and decided the best course of action would be if the two of you would combine your business plans. When I called him, he sounded very excited and was quite sure you'd be on board. Frankly, I'm a bit surprised at your reaction."

"Unfortunately, Tucker had failed to inform me of his interest in the property, so you can understand my surprise and frustration."

"I was trying to help." Her dark blue gaze shot daggers at him and she resumed her proud, defiant tilt of the chin. Damn, she could be stubborn. Withdrawing his offer was the best decision.

"So, now here we are, neither of you have signed the papers and the committee wants to have this wrapped up by tomorrow, Christmas Eve."

"Fine, I'm ready to sign the papers if I am the sole recipient of the bid."

"Just give it to her, Arthur," Tucker said.

There was no point sticking around. Liza was still too stubborn to acknowledge that he only tried to help and, honestly, he was exhausted.

Since the night of the ball, he'd had little sleep; trying to get some shut-eye on the camper's hard, narrow bed while visions of Liza handing back the key made sleep impossible. He pushed out of his chair and grabbed the doorknob, but stopped with Arthur's next words.

"If you walk out now, Tucker, we will award the bid to Bridges Enterprises."

"What?" Liza rose out of her chair as she blurted out her indignation.

"Weren't you two listening? We can't pass up the revenue the gas station will generate. Unless the two of you go in together and create both a gallery and a pub with extra retail space, the committee has no other choice than to give it to them."

"And tear down the castle?"

"Yes, Liza, and tear down the castle."

He sagged against the door and Liza flopped back in her chair. She wouldn't even look at him—how could they begin to work together to save the castle?

"Since we know neither of you want to see the castle torn down, I suggest you work this thing out between the two of you. We'll give you a few minutes to discuss it."

With that, the committee stood up and shuffled out of the room, leaving them facing each other across a cold, empty table with just the ticking of the wall clock filling the silence. Liza kept her arms folded across her chest as she rocked back and forth in the leather chair. Tucker drummed his fingers on the table, creating the sound of a horse's hooves in full gallop. If only he could run away right now.

"You start." Liza was the first to break the stand-off.

"What do you want me to say?"

"How about you tell me why you kept this from me? Why didn't you discuss any of this with me? Why you lied to me, made me believe you thought I could make the gallery a success? Why you—"

"I know you can make the gallery a success."

"Then why were we granted the bid together?"

"You heard Arthur. They were going to give the bid to Bridges Enterprises unless we formed a partnership. The gallery alone wouldn't provide as many jobs or create as much revenue for the town. I thought I was helping. I thought you'd be happy."

"I just don't know why you didn't tell me you had submitted a bid."

"I was going to tell you right before you told me. But we had just made love and everything was so perfect."

She flinched when he said the word but, damn it, everything was perfect until his big surprise blew up in his face.

"You were so excited about your plans. I didn't want to mess up. Didn't want to get shot down again."

"Shot down?"

"Yes, shot down. I tried to salvage the situation, but it looks like you and me together just wasn't in the cards." He stood up, slipped into his coat, and pulled an envelope from the inside pocket. "This is a copy of the letter I wrote to the board, withdrawing my interest in the castle project." He tossed the envelope across the table and reached for the door. "You need to make your decision by tomorrow. Merry Christmas."

TWENTY-THREE

Tucker slammed the door behind him, making the window blinds rattle and sending a spike through her heart. He was so angry, so defeated when he stormed out of the room. All of this was finally starting to make sense: he didn't want to upset her with his own plans so he tried to back out. But the city would give the bid to Bridges unless Tucker and Liza teamed up. She wouldn't mind working with him and was willing to compromise on the site plan.

But she had been hoping for more than a business partnership. Before he pulled out that key, she was excited at the prospect of a proposal, and even though it was the "key to his heart," he still hadn't told her he loved her. Virginia seemed to think he was in love with her, but he hadn't uttered the words.

Liza slit open the sealed envelope and unfolded the letter, written in Tucker's chicken scratch on Misty Mountain stationery.

Dear Members of the Castle Property Committee,

It is with deep regret that I officially and finally withdraw my bid to restore the castle and build additional retail outlets along the east end of Main Street. As you know, I thought the castle would make an impressive English pub and the adjoining storefronts would add to the already beautiful downtown. But, once I learned of Liza Fisk's better idea to turn the castle into an art gallery and sculpture garden, I knew it was best to withdraw my bid. Since it does not appear Ms. Fisk is interested in your idea to join forces and form a lasting partnership with me, I have no other option than to rescind my offer. I stand stalwart in encouraging you to award the bid to Ms. Fisk so she can realize her dream and that of her great-grandfather.

More than anything, it is my hope that the castle remains standing. Therefore, I will donate the proceeds obtained from the recent sale of my house to one of the city's many worthwhile programs to offset the potential loss of revenue from the gallery project, and will continue to do so on an annual basis. However, I am more than confident that in a short time, Ms. Fisk's venture will generate the kind of tax revenue and employment opportunities you had envisioned. Thank you for this opportunity.

Sincerely,

Tucker J. Callum

"You big oaf!" She ripped the letter in half and dropped her face in her hands. Why didn't he tell her this?

The conference room door creaked open and her head popped up, hoping Tucker had returned.

"How are you doing, honey?" Virginia slipped into the room, carrying a cardboard tube, and shut the door behind her. Liza's heart sank. There was so much she wanted to say to Tucker.

"Terrible. Did you see this letter Tucker wrote to the committee?"

"I did. I hated to see him give up on his idea, but I understand why he did it." Virginia eased into the chair beside her and laid the package on the table. She folded her wrinkled hands over her belly and rocked back and forth.

"What's that?"

"Those are the sketches Tucker originally submitted."

"Can I see them?"

"Sure, honey."

Virginia shimmied off the lid of the cardboard tube, shook the contents onto the table, and rolled out Tucker's blueprints. Liza drew in a sharp breath as a beautiful streetscape unfolded before her with the castle as its centerpiece. The additional retail spaces flanking either side of the castle were an extension of the granite fortress, but in varying heights and styles similar to other downtown buildings. She flipped to the next page to find a sketch of the rear of the castle where a lovely, landscaped beer garden was planned. The remaining pages were of detailed plans for the interiors of the castle and retail spaces. His idea would be a wonderful addition to the town.

"I can't believe he withdrew."

"Your happiness is more important to him than making a bunch of money. That boy loves you."

"So, why hasn't he ever told me? Don't get me wrong, he's wonderful to me and says the sweetest things, but he's never told me he loves me."

"I asked him the same thing."

She snatched Virginia's hands away from the blueprints and pulled the two of them down into their chairs. She looked into Virginia's caring eyes as her heart thumped like a bass drum. "You talked to Tucker about me?"

"I sure did. After you left the ball, I pulled him aside."

"What did he say?"

"He was distraught. He thought he had done the right thing by allowing us to combine your bids, but then you stormed out."

"Yeah, but what about the 'he loves me' part."

"That's the part that was a little confusing. He was pacing in a circle, rubbing the top of his head and muttering things like 'I should've told her' and 'I wanted to tell her I love her, but was afraid to jinx it.' Something about a curse and he didn't want to mess up the perfect thing you had going. I tell you, honey, he had me worried. Thankfully, Brody took him home and got him settled."

"Oh, no."

"Does any of that make sense to you, because it sure didn't to me?"

"Yes!" She jumped out of the chair and plastered a loud kiss on Virginia's cheek. "It makes perfect sense. I've got to go." She gathered her coat in her hand and stuffed the ripped letter in her purse. As she reached for the door, she turned back around.

"Can I take that with me?"

"Sure, honey, but what are you going to tell the committee?"

She hugged Tucker's blueprints to her chest as she opened the door.

"Tell them I promise to be here bright and early the day after Christmas to sign the papers. If things go my way, everyone will get what they want."

Twenty-Four

Liza jiggled the key in the entry door to the community center activity room until it clicked. She stepped into the darkness and flipped on the lights. The Mistletoe Ball decorations had yet to be removed. Decorated Christmas trees still lined the perimeter, strings of lights were still draped from corner to corner, and the enormous ball of artificial evergreens still hung over the dance floor.

"I see you beat me here." Travis let the door bang behind him as he shrugged out of his coat.

"Thanks for coming down here on such short notice. I wasn't sure if I could figure out how to use the projector or how to lower the screen."

"Sure thing. Let me get the equipment fired up."

"And, while you do that, I'll light the trees."

She rushed around plugging cords into outlets, lighting the strands overhead and on the trees until a thousand tiny bulbs glowed in the waning Christmas Eve daylight. She had barely slept last night for thinking of how she would apologize to Tucker and share her plans for the castle. This morning after her first cup of coffee, Travis popped into her head as the right accomplice for her surprise.

"Come on over here and let me show you where to plug in your thumb drive," he called from inside a closet. She hurried across the room to where a tall stack of electronics blinked with so many colorful lights it made her head spin.

"I'll never figure this out."

"You don't have to. I'll get everything ready. Give me the thumb drive." He plugged the drive into a computer and tapped a few keys. "It's all set. Here take the remote. When you're ready just push this button and then this one."

"What about the screen?"

"I'm going to lower it now. Thought it would make it easier on you."

Yes, it was better to have everything set up than for her to fumble around nervously once Tucker arrived. She wanted her presentation to make a big impact.

"Ready for me to call Tucker?"

"Yes, but how are you going to get him here?"

"He was supposed to pick me up on his way to Brody and Kate's." He pulled out his cell phone and hit a button. "I'll put it on speaker. Watch and learn from the master."

Within seconds, Tucker answered the call. "Travis, what's up?"

"Have you left yet?"

"I'm about three minutes from your place."

"Hey, change of plans. I had to stop over at the community center to check the furnace."

"Something wrong?"

"Not really. It was giving me a fit the other day when I was working on it. Just wanted to make sure the place was still nice and toasty."

"No problem. I'll be there soon."

He clicked off the call and took a bow. "And that's how you trick your buddy."

"Thank you, Travis. I couldn't have done it without your help." She gave him a hug and kissed him on the cheek before pushing him toward the door.

"Here's your hat, what's your hurry?" He chuckled as he slipped his arms inside his coat.

"Sorry, but I need a minute alone before he gets here."

"Okay, I hear you. I hope everything goes okay."

"You and me both. Bye, Travis."

She stood at the door and watched as Travis's truck pulled out of sight. She hurried back into the activity room and dimmed the overhead lights, leaving just the decorative bulbs twinkling. With a flip of a switch, spotlights shone on the mistletoe ball as it spun above the dance floor. Soft, instrumental Christmas music floated on the air.

Headlights beamed across the wall announcing Tucker's arrival, so Liza hid behind one of the Christmas trees. Her plan had to work. More than anything she wanted to prove to him she was no longer frightened of happiness, especially this time of year. It was time she started creating her own happiness rather than letting curses dictate her holidays.

"Travis?" Tucker's voice rang out from the community center's foyer. "You still here?"

He pulled the door open and leaned his head into the room. "Hey, Travis."

Liza drew in a deep breath, crossed her fingers behind her back, and stepped from behind the tree.

"Travis isn't here."

"Liza." He took a step back and for a second she thought he would leave. "What are you doing here?" He walked into the room, letting the door close behind him. Golden beams of light highlighted the confusion on his face.

"I left the Mistletoe Ball so abruptly I thought maybe we could go back to that night."

"Why?"

"I feel like I owe you a better ending. I mean, you always wanted to play Mr. Claus and I sort of messed up the finale of your reign."

"What are you up to?"

A sharp pain burned under her diaphragm and she fought the urge to double over. He was still upset with her. The way his arms were crossed over his chest and his eyes glared at her, it might be too late. She dug her fist into her chest and pushed the button on the remote control.

"What's this?" He stepped farther into the room and looked up at the screen covered in a bright, white light.

"I have something to show you." She hit another button and Tucker's sketch of the castle-turned-pub and outlying retail spaces covered the screen, but with a few modifications. Instead of the castle sitting front and center, it was now on the west end of the lot and an identical stone structure sat on the east side. In between were three additional retail spaces. Over the castle door was a sign that read *The Camelot Gallery* and over its twin building were the words *The Lifted Curse Pub*.

Tucker stepped closer to the screen with his mouth agape and his eyes mere slits. Why didn't he say something? Anything? Did he like it? Did he hate it? Did he hate her?

"Who drew this?"

"I did. What do you think?"

He shoved his hands into his front pockets and continued to stare at the screen. Maybe if she showed him the other sketches, he'd say something. She clicked a button on the remote and her drawing of the back of the complex covered the screen. Behind the gallery was a smaller version of her sculpture garden, six parking spaces were drawn in back of the retail stores, and a grassy space dotted with picnic tables sat outside the pub.

"Well?" She took a few tentative steps toward him, wringing her hands as she watched the screen's reflection dance over his face.

"Huh."

"Damn it, Tucker." She closed the distance between them, shoving her hands into his shoulder and knocking him off balance. "Is that all you're going to say?" She perched her fists on her hips and glared at him. "Do you like it or don't you?"

He turned slowly toward her with a wry grin on his face. His eyes trailed down the length of her body, taking in the beaded gown she wore to the ball, and back up again.

"You look awful cute tonight."

Of course, she looked good. She's spent the better part of the afternoon getting ready, and even though she was frustrated right now, she was pleased with his sexy smile and smoldering gaze. All her efforts had paid off in that department. Now, what about the castle?

"Thank you, but you haven't said anything about the sketches."

"So, you get the original castle and I get a replica?"

"It doesn't matter, I'll take the replica. Just tell me you like my idea."

"I like you." He took a dramatic giant step toward her and swept her into his arms.

"I'm glad. I wasn't so sure after the way I acted at the ball."

"And the way you wouldn't answer my calls or texts for the past few days."

"I'm sorry. I know it was juvenile, but I was so upset."

"I know, babe, and I'm sorry." He drew her in close and kissed her temple. She had missed being held tight in his strong arms, feeling safe and loved. Virginia had said he loved her and she believed it, but she needed to hear the words. She kept her hands on his broad shoulders, and stepped back, putting a few inches between them so she could see his face.

"What do you think of the name of the pub? You can change it if you want, but—"

"Are you trying to tell me you no longer believe in the curse?"

"Right now, with your arms around me? No. I don't."

"Good, because I have something important to say to you."

Finally, he was going to speak those three little words she'd been longing to hear. Tell her he loved her and wanted to marry her and have babies. She would spend the rest of her life with her very best friend.

"I can't live in that little camper another night. My back is killing me and this morning I woke up with the worst charley horse."

"Tucker!" Tears filled her eyes as she flatted her hands against his chest, fighting against his ironclad hold. He threw back his head with a hearty laugh and gripped her butt in his hands.

"I'm sorry, I couldn't resist. You were looking up at me with those gorgeous, blue puppy dog eyes and I just had to—"

"You're so mean."

"I'm sorry. What were you expecting me to say? Hmm?"

He skimmed his hand up the back of her dress, setting off a thousand sparks, and cupped her neck, rubbing his thumb slowly against her skin.

His lips brushed over her forehead, to each cheek, and then touched her mouth as soft as a whisper.

"Did you want me to say I love you?" He gathered her face in his hands and kissed her with a bit more passion. "Because I do." This time his mouth was more demanding, smothering her lips in a long, sumptuous kiss.

After several breathless moments, he ended the kiss with a quick peck to the tip of her nose. "I love you, Liza. Always have. Always will."

"And I love you."

He bent down for another kiss, but she put her hand over his mouth. There was something they needed to do.

"Come with me." She grabbed his hands and, keeping her eyes on his handsome face, the face she planned to wake up to for the rest of her life, she pulled him into the center of the room. "We still need to kiss under the mistletoe as Mr. and Mrs. Claus."

Centered under the mistletoe, he circled his arms around her waist and lifted her off the ground. With his long, slow kiss, all her fears and worries disappeared. The curse was forever lifted. They stayed in each other's arms, swaying to the music and locked in a kiss for so long that Liza nearly forgot she still had one more thing to show him. When the kiss ended, she pushed a button on the remote.

The same sketch with the castle on one corner and the pub on the other lit up the screen, but this time strings of white lights lined each window and along the roof. Small Christmas trees adorned each shop window and evergreen wreaths with red bows decorated the doors of the pub and gallery.

"What's this?"

"This is what our little block will look like the night of the winter street festival."

"It's very…Christmassy."

"Isn't it though?"

"I'm surprised."

She wrapped her arms around his neck and pressed her nose to his. "You shouldn't be. Thanks to you, the curse is lifted and I'm starting to like Christmas again."

"You are?"

"A little." She pinched her fingers together. "As long as I spend all my Christmases with you from now on."

"You can guarantee it."

She gathered his face in her hands and looked into his dark, chocolate eyes. "I love you, Tucker."

"Oh, babe, I love you, too."

They kissed under the mistletoe to the sound of "White Christmas," and for the first time Liza thought Christmas was the most magical time of year.

Acknowledgements

What fun it was for me to return to Highland Springs and bring you Liza and Tucker's story. It goes without saying that I couldn't have completed this book without the help of some very smart, talented, generous people.

It was Rebecca Heyman who guided me through the early developmental edits and inspired the title Whatever We Are. She has worked with me from the very beginning, and I can't thank her enough for all she's taught me.

Thank you to Jessica Snyder, whom I met over lunch during a Washington Romance Writers meeting, for doing the developmental and line edits on the revised story. Her keen insights into romance made the manuscript shine.

It was such a pleasure to work with Beth Balberchak, another Washington Romance Writers member, who proofread the final version.

Whatever We Are is the third book for which the amazingly talented Shona Andrew of spikyshooz.com has designed the cover. She's such a joy to work with and always makes the design process easy.

Thank you to Kat Sheridan for her marketing skills, and a special thanks to the Ebook Formatting Fairies for preparing the book for publication.

If the description of Liza's scar made you a little squeamish, you can thank my friend Holli Lindenfelser, BSN. She is my go-to medical professional for all things related to injuries, diseases, and anything else health related. Thanks, Holli!

Just like in past books, I've used my friend's and family's names without their permission, and I am so happy they are all still talking to me—especially my daughter, Liza. When I introduced Liza Fisk in Whatever You Say, I hadn't intended to write a book with her as the main character. But there was something about this quirky, pink-haired (or blue or purple) artist that really captured my heart, and I just felt she deserved her own book. Thanks to the real Liza for the use of her beautiful name.

Finally, I want to thank my friends who have supported and encouraged me since embarking on this writing journey. And, most especially, I thank my husband Pat, son Tom, and daughter Liza for their continued love and support.

Thank you for reading *Whatever We Are*. If you enjoyed it, please help other readers find this book:

- Write a review on the site where you purchased the book.
- Keep up with news of upcoming releases by signing up for my newsletter at www.leighfleming.com.
- Like my Facebook page: www.facebook.com/leighhflemingauthor.
- Follow me on Twitter: www.twitter.com/leighhfleming1

Ready to Read More?

Check Out This Excerpt of **Stay Hidden**, a romantic suspense by Leigh Fleming, coming soon!

Chapter One

Riley strolled down the tree-lined street, past Victorian houses and Craftsman bungalows, as the sun sank low behind the rooftops and the spicy sweetness of blooming lilacs filled the air. Today had been bright and sunny, but now there was a nip in the breeze that made her draw her sweater tighter around the middle as she walked home from Beautiful Blooms. A dog barked from a backyard; she knew it was Tiny, the Putnam's Rottweiler, who often escaped his yard and found his way to hers. She would give him a long scratch under his fuzzy chin and feed him a biscuit before he went on his way.

Just the thought of never seeing that smelly, lovable dog again made her eyes water.

She had stayed too long. Six months in one place was time enough to be found. Today, after her phone lit up with *Unknown Caller* for the umpteenth time, she decided it was definitely time to go. This weekend was Kate and Brody's wedding, which she couldn't miss since she was in charge of the flowers, but Monday morning, she would pack up her car before the sun came up and head to another town.

As she rounded the corner onto Maple Street, the sound of an idling truck drew her attention away from the beautiful pink dogwoods in the Finton's yard. Over her shoulder she saw an old Ford cruising slowly down the street. It looked a lot like Brody's truck, but the color wasn't right and his didn't have a dent in the grill. When the truck sped up and the driver-side window lowered, Riley's heart rate tripled. She picked up her pace, looking around for anyone who might be outside, watering flowers or rocking on their porch, as the thumping in her chest made it hard to breath.

Four more houses and she would be in her front yard, just steps from safety. She spared another glance for the truck and noticed a plaid-sleeved elbow jutting from the driver-side window. She was practically running now, her hips aching as she drew within a hundred yards of her house.

"Hey," the drive yelled.

It was him. She would recognize that voice anywhere. How had he found her? She had been so careful this time—kept a low profile, only paid in cash, replaced her track phone every couple of months. There was no way he could have traced her to Highland Springs.

With another look over her shoulder, she nearly lost her breath when the driver leaned his head out the window, drawing alongside her. His dark, wavy bangs flopped over his forehead, looking so much like—

"Excuse me."

Riley couldn't wait another second. He could be out of that truck and tackle her to the ground in a flash. She ran the final few yards to her porch. Her hand shook so violently she couldn't get her key in the lock.

"Hey, can you tell me how to get to College Avenue?"

This time when she cast a look over her shoulder, Riley didn't see a memory, but a dark-haired teenager who looked nothing like *him*.

"I'm sorry, Miss? I can't find College Avenue."

He didn't even sound like him.

"Oh, um, okay…" Her mouth was so dry, she could barely speak. "It's um…" Her arm felt weighted down as she pointed up the street. "It's two more blocks that way."

"Great. Thanks. Sorry to bother you."

Riley sagged against the screen door as the old pick-up pulled away. She trudged to the edge of her porch, where she sank onto the top step and dropped her head into quivering hands. Another false alarm. Her mind, yet again, playing tricks on her. When would she stop seeing his face, hearing his voice? Not until he slipped up and was finally punished for his laundry-list of crimes. Until then, she would keep facing the fear she'd had since leaving Kentucky. She'd keep feeling it—and she'd keep running.

Riley's heart skipped when a muffled meow floated from deep inside a blue hydrangea bush, its owner an orange striped tabby who leaped onto her steps. He slinked against her shins and dipped behind her knees, then forced his way onto her lap.

"Hello, Tiger. Not a good day, I'm afraid." The cat belonged to Sam Smiley across the street, and often came for the kibble Riley kept on hand for his frequent visits. While she stroked the cat's soft, fluffy coat, she replayed the scene over and over, in rhythm with Tiger's rumbling purr, reminding herself it was just an illusion. He hadn't found her. Not this time.

Legs heavy from the adrenaline that had coursed through her system, she couldn't imagine standing right now—let alone running anywhere safe. She forced herself to take deep, steady breaths, stroking Tiger's fur in rhythm with her inhales and exhales, until her heartbeat slowed and her tremors subsided. The evening breeze helped dry her damp forehead, lifting her hair to cool the back of her neck. She had to get herself under control. Her luck only had to hold out another few days, and then she could put her fears to rest—at least for a little while.

About the Author

Twenty years ago Leigh Fleming vowed to write a book someday and her goal finally came to fruition in 2013. Since the day she first sat down at the computer to write, she has been hard at work creating unique characters facing life's challenges, but who are always rewarded with their happy ending. When she's not writing in her windowless office, she enjoys reading, travelling, scrapbooking, and spending time with friends.

Leigh is a member of Romance Writers of America and the Washington Romance Writers chapter. She lives in Martinsburg, West Virginia, with her husband, Patrick, and her deaf French Bulldog Napoleon, and is mom to adult children, Tom and Liza.

www.ingramcontent.com/pod-product-compliance
Lightning Source LLC
Chambersburg PA
CBHW071908220626
47052CB00002B/262